MW01244910

Other Works by Juana Culhane

The Celestial Monster:
Two Collections of Stories
(NY, Spuyten Duyvil, 2008)

The Revelations of Dr. Purcell:
Stories from the Life of a Psychotherapist
(West Virginia, University Editions, 1992)

The Shadow of the Cat-Goddess
(in The Theory and Practice of Self-Psychology,
NY, Brunner Mazel, 1986)

The Headless Toy Soldiers:
The Terrorization of a Patient by Unsoothing Introjects
(in Psychotherapy and the Terrorized Patient,
NY, Haworth Press, 1985)

Bird on the Wing:

Travels of the Self

JUANA CULHANE

SPUYTEN DUYVIL

New York City

ISBN 978-1-933132-90-7

Cover painting by Panama Campbell

Author Photograph by Mara Ceglia

Library of Congress Cataloging-in-Publication Data

Culhane, Juana.
Bird on the wing : travels of the self / Juana Culhane.
p. cm.
ISBN 978-1-933132-90-7
I. Title.
PS3603.U56B57 2011
813'.6--dc22

2011016976

Come, fill the Cup, and in the Fire of Spring
Your Winter Garment of Repentance fling:
The Bird of Time has but a little way
To flutter—and the Bird is on the Wing.

THE RUBAIYAT OF OMAR KHAYYAM

THIS BOOK IS DEDICATED TO ALL

WHO HAVE TOUCHED MY LIFE

WITH THEIR CARING.

CONTENTS

VAGABONDS

The first rays of the sun emerged from behind the mountains, from behind the old volcanoes. Mother and daughter walked arm in arm on the dirt road—Benita not yet thirty, Joanna eight years old. "See mama," Joanna exclaimed, breaking away and lifting her arms up high to the sky, "This is what I wanted to see with you, only with you!"

"Fine thing, getting me up so early!" Benita wrapped her sweater more tightly around herself. After a moment, she added, "But then you seldom ask anything of me; you've grown up so fast, too fast!"

The grassy mounds along the sides of the road still held onto tiny silvery globules, remnants of the nightly rain typical of the Costa Rican climate. Ahead they saw a brightly painted oxcart parked on a narrow path leading off from the main road. As they approached they saw a bundle of rags under it; as they passed, it stirred. When they were a few steps beyond it, they heard singing, "God is sweet. He smells of soft clouds. I smell of dew. Oh how sweet we smell!" Looking back they saw a woman standing up, leaning against the side of the wagon braiding her long white hair, smiling to herself. As they watched, the woman folded up her rags into a neat pile. They saw her pick up a packet with a shiny wrapping that had been under her bedding. She opened it, nibbling at some of the insides before closing the packet again. Then suddenly she went skipping down the road, away from them.

"Mama, where is she going?" Joanna took her mother's arm.

"I don't know, my sweet. Let's go, darling."

They walked onwards but Joanna kept stopping, looking back, "Where is she going? Does she have a home somewhere else, a real home with a roof? Could she be going to that little white church way up on the hill?"

"Don't keep looking back! I thought you wanted me to take you to the Fabrega Farm to get sugarcane—we'll never get there at this rate!"

Joanna's face crinkled up. The mother hated it when Joanna looked like a little old woman—it was as if she'd lost her child to another being, a demon who had swallowed her up.

"I can't help it; I don't understand why she sings when she has no home."

The mother sighed, gripping her daughter's arm even more tightly, "My sweet, a home doesn't always have a roof or even a floor for that matter."

"Or walls either?" Joanna queried.

"That's right," Benita murmured wondering where the conversation was going, knowing how unpredictable her daughter was. Out there, in the middle of nowhere, she wouldn't be able to send her to her room, if she should get too intense, too overwrought, taxing Benita's every nerve cell.

"But where is that place that's a home, yet isn't?"

Benita took a deep breath trying to remain calm, "It's where you feel you belong."

"What does that mean, mama?"

"To belong means you're in a place where you're loved and therefore where you are happy."

"Oh," Joanna began, "I have a roof, a floor, and many walls."

"Yes, you do, mi hijita, my dearest, special daughter," Benita put her arm around Joanna's shoulders drawing her close to herself.

Joanna pulled away, "But mama I don't have a home!"

"What! What are you saying?"

"I don't belong, you don't love me! You're always telling me how bad I am, how wild, how shameless! You call me traviesa, mala, disverguenza!"

Benita stopped walking; she faced Joanna, her olive-toned skin becoming flushed, her soft features becoming outlined with hard creases. She shook Joanna by the shoulders, "That's because you always spoil everything; you always end up making me furious! But I do love you, do you hear me? I do love you! You don't know what it means to *not* be loved, to *not* be happy, to truly *not* belong!"

Joanna pulled away from her mother's strong hands, "Tell me then, tell me, what do you mean?"

"Oh, what am I going to do with you! Your papa has totally spoiled you, giving you all those books, talking to you for hours, turning your head, making you think you're grownup, making you think you're better than I! Let me tell you, you're just a little girl, a child with too many words in your little adorable bloated head!"

Tearing off her green jacket, her favorite, one that she had picked out herself in the market, Joanna tossed it to the ground. Then she ran back down the road in the direction from where they'd come, her dress spreading out around her like the wings on a fly. Benita ran after her, her body too opulent for her short legs, for her little feet, "Stop, stop. Amorcito, please stop!"

Eventually Joanna stopped, sitting down on a grassy mound on the side of the road. As the mother approached she asked, "Why don't *you* talk to me? Why don't *you* give me things?"

Benita answered in a breathless voice, "But I do! I make all your dresses, your organza aprons, even the ribbons for your braids. I embroider your socks, trimming them with lace. Don't tell me you forget how you prance around showing off your lacy ankles!"

"But mama, you don't talk to me! You don't want me to talk to you either! You hate my questions, you hate so much about me!"

"That's nonsense!" Then walking slowly towards Joanna and cautiously placing her hands on her shoulders, Benita asked, "Now, what is it you want to talk about?"

"What you said about not being loved, not really having a home," Joanna answered moving her head towards her mother's chest while embracing her.

"But, mi hija, mi hijita, that's what *you* said about

yourself and it made me angry and sad."

"Mama, no, *you* said I didn't know anything about—"

"That's right, Joancita, you have *no* right to complain. You have everything! You're living the life of a princess; you rule over everyone!"

Joanna jumped to her feet, tearing at one of her braids, unwinding it, throwing the silk ribbon to the ground, her face crumbling as she sobbed.

"Oh, *Dios mio*, what is wrong with you? What am I going to do with you?' Benita wrung her hands.

With half of her hair loose, long, flowing, Joanna grabbed her mother's hand and began to skip down the road, "Come, mamacita, let's see where the woman went, the one with the long white hair, the singing woman."

Benita laughed, allowing herself to be pulled along, relieved Joanna was herself again. They returned to the oxcart where the woman had left her bedding, her rags. They climbed up a narrow hilly path until they reached the white church. Joanna disengaged herself running ahead. Tugging the heavy wooden door open she waited for Benita.

The inside of the church was dark, cold; the windows were small and high on the walls, the floor a pebbly cement. The one room was filled with many rows of narrow wooden benches. Only the far end held any color; up on the altar stood a painted life-size statue of Jesus Christ hanging on a cross, emaciated, bleeding, tormented expression on his face. As mother and daughter walked down the long narrow aisle they saw the woman kneeling in front of him, her leftover packet of food at his feet.

"Eat, eat!" they heard her implore, "You need it more than I; you still suffer pinned to that cross while I am free."

Joanna ran up to the woman, Benita trying to hold her back, "He can't eat, don't you see!"

Showing no surprise that the girl had addressed her, the woman smiled, not replying. Benita approached her, "Please forgive my daughter, señora; we don't mean to intrude. I'm certain el Cristo appreciates your generosity."

"But mama—," Joanna began.

"Come on, Joancita, let's go!" Benita insisted.

The woman stood up approaching Joanna, "Child, you are right and you are wrong. He doesn't eat because he is always dying, but he *could* eat, he *will* eat when he's resurrected, when he comes to life again."

"Why is he dying? He is not old!" Joanna exclaimed.

"We are all dying, my child, but one day we will be alive forever and ever! But we have to be good, right mama?" The woman turned towards Benita.

"Yes," mumbled Benita, taken aback, embarrassed, still trying to draw Joanna away towards the door.

Once outside Joanna exploded with questions, "Are we really dying, mama? Is that why I feel I don't have a home, that you don't love me? Do you feel the same way, without a home, without papa's love, without my love? Did *your* mama love you? Did she? Did she?" Joanna's voice became louder and louder.

"Hush, hush, you're giving me a headache!" Benita almost screamed wanting to cover Joanna's mouth.

Not able to reach her daughter's face, she sighed and continued, "Mama had a hard life, always working to keep a roof over our head, especially when papa was away. We lived far from here, in another country, a place not as quiet as this one. We all had to pitch in and work hard. Sometimes we had to sacrifice ourselves for the family—you can't even begin to comprehend—"

"Tell me, what sacrifices?"

"You wouldn't understand, you shouldn't have to!"

"Tell me! I won't go another step till you tell me!" Joanna begged.

Embracing her daughter, continuing to walk slowly, Benita spoke hesitantly, "When I was five years older than you are now, thirteen, my mama took me to live in another home for one year in return for food and money for our whole village."

Joanna didn't understand; she was choking on more and more questions, some of them not able to be formed into words, "What did you have to do?" she asked trying to escape her mother's strong grip around her shoulders, Benita's fingers digging into her flesh.

"That's it! You asked and I answered; we're not going to talk about it anymore!"

"Why not, mama?"

"Because I said so! I keep telling papa not to tell you too much; you twist everything around!"

Still pinned together in a painful embrace they walked in silence all the way back to their home. Then as Benita was about to unlock the wrought iron gate that protected their lush garden, their beautiful stone house, Joanna asked cautiously in a solemn voice, "You remember when you sent me on that boat trip with papa, didn't you send me away to another home, didn't you give me away the way your mama gave you away?"

Benita dropped her key ring, her face pale, her lips trembling, she stood transfixed on the street unable to lead her daughter through the gate and into the garden.

BOY WITH RED ROOSTER

It was Easter Sunday; the loft apartment was full of people who mainly stood around the buffet table eating, drinking, talking and laughing. Nearby, separated by an open archway, there was an almost deserted sitting area. A large man sat on a low couch, his stomach pointed toward the ceiling as he leaned backwards—legs wide apart, feet splayed out which now and then tapped on the floor, first one foot and then the other. His head was large but went well with his Buddha belly. It was difficult to make out what shape his features were because they kept moving around on the rough terrain of his face, dark, restless, ageless, yet aged. A big-boned statuesque woman returned from the buffet table with a plate of sliced meats, salad and hardboiled eggs in a creamy horseradish. She approached the couch, "Here Max, eat this, you've had a rough day!" Her breasts never jiggled this way or that; they had no life of their own.

"Thanks mama." Max sat up straight grasping for the plate with staccato movements, looking wildly around the room seeking affirmation he was doing the right thing.

Veronica turned to Joanna, the only other person in that area, "We had to dismantle his show today; what a job!"

Seated across from Max, Joanna asked, "What kind of a show?"

Veronica came to sit on a straight chair next to Joanna, "Max is a prominent artist, right Max?"

Guiltily wiping his mouth with a napkin Max stammered, "Yes mama, if you say so."

Veronica reached into her shoulder bag and handed Joanna a brochure. On the cover was a boy holding a red rooster. The youngster wore a floppy blue hat that seemed made of velvet, a bright yellow tunic reaching down to his hips. The picture ended there. The rooster was long, thin, his radiant red feathers hiding the boy's hands as well as part of his own crown and beak. The boy's face startled Joanna, green eyes looking horrified, a rabbit's nose almost twitching, a pink mouth opened with no teeth, mouthing a scream.

"It's so real, so alive! Joanna exclaimed looking at Veronica's face for the first time—enchanting white teeth, as unreal as her breasts; were her eyes authentic? Joanna let herself become drawn into them, into the golden brown speckled orbs. Where were they leading her? The jungles of the western hemisphere, its deserts? Or were they leading her to a special room where the crystal floor reflected a multiplicity of eyes, a room where a strange being reigned with a lion's mane, with the body of a calf, with long arms flapping like wings but with the face of a man-woman, a god.

Joanna turned away abruptly, shaking her head to awaken herself from what she recognized as one of her fleeting fugue states, a kind of a waking dream. She knew how to bring herself down to earth; she had only to concentrate on her bodily pain in most of her joints from the neck down to her toes. Sighing, Joanna stretched and then bent each leg, laughing a little, "Forgive me, it's just this goddamn arthritis of mine! It's not the old age type; I've had it since I was very young!"

Veronica looked sympathetic, "You poor dear—" and shaking her head she turned to look at Max. Seeing a white splotch on his dark shirt she rose to her feet, rushing over to clean him up. He mumbled, "Thank you; I'm sorry."

As Veronica leaned over her son, Joanna noticed the beauty of the long legs tightly wrapped in leather jeans, firm muscles—calves, thighs, buttocks, waist; no misplaced flesh anywhere. Was Veronica purposely exhibiting herself to Joanna? No, not in a sexual way but to show off the superiority of her limbs as if she had sculpted herself. Perhaps she thought Joanna had sculpted herself also. Had Max created himself, his floppiness, his disjointedness? Joanna was reminded of what her psychotherapist had once told her, that as a beautiful model she was a decorative object, as a teacher-counselor a useful object, and finally as a writer she created her own objects, her own world.

When Veronica returned to the chair next to Joanna she made a mock sign of fatigue, "Work never ends for a single mom!"

Joanna would have thought she was referring to the caring of a young child, not the caring of a grown-up man of around thirty years of age, "What happened to the father?" she asked.

"He died seven years ago under suspicious circumstances as they say!"

"May I ask what happened?" Joanna continued, savoring a disc of toast dotted with black caviar, aware she was emboldened by the champagne.

"He disappeared overboard on a cruise on the Baltic Sea."

"Were you and Max on the same ship?"

"Yes, but Henri had walked off on his own."

Looking Joanna up and down, Veronica asked, "May I ask *you* something?"

"Yes, go ahead."

"Tell me, how has your disease affected your love life?"

"Well, I've had three husbands and lovers between marriages—no one complained!"

"But didn't you resent what was happening to you? Didn't you hate losing control?"

Joanna thought for a second, "I've asked myself, which would I prefer—to be a victim or a perpetrator, I couldn't stand causing harm to others!"

Seeing Veronica's perplexed expression, Joanna laughed, wondering why she'd said what she said. She must be more drunk than she thought. Come to think of it, she'd had a couple of champagnes before settling down on her chair and then she'd just had two more with the tiny black eggs.

"But why one or the other?" Veronica persisted.

Glibly, Joanna answered, "There's usually the big one and the little one, parent-child, teacher-student, doctor-patient and so on.

"You talk as if your illness provides you with brakes so you don't over-speed, so you don't become too full of yourself! What must you think of me! *I* have to be in total control to the extent of being a total bitch!"

Joanna laughed saying nothing further. Veronica gracefully leaped to her feet, "Well, you must excuse me. I have to circulate. I'm drumming up support for Max's work!"

Joanna was alone with Max once again. Somehow she liked it this way. Max looked content also, leaning back once again but this time his facial features and his toes were relaxed. She wondered what he was thinking, what he was seeing up on the ceiling. Was he aware of her presence?

Suddenly he sat up, addressing her, "What's your name?"

"Joanna."

"Happy to know you!" And Max rubbed his hands, first one, then the other, then he rubbed one knee, then the other, finally placing his hands flat upon his belly, still looking at her. His eyes were upon her, yet they were not; they glared above her forehead, around her sleek hairline but she knew he saw her clearly.

"You liked my rooster?"

"Yes, and the boy too!"

He continued, "You don't think the boy killed the rooster?"

"I didn't know the rooster was dead."

"Yes, dead dead rooster, did the boy kill it?"

Joanna smiled, "I really don't know; after all you're the artist; did you paint a rooster that had been killed by the boy?"

"Don't know, only hands know," and he looked at his hands, holding them in front of his face.

"What do your hands say?" Joanna asked half in jest.

"Hands don't talk!" Max was indignant, "Don't make fun of me!" His hands clenched tightly into enormous fists.

"I'm sorry but sometimes I *do* believe that parts of our bodies do speak or perhaps I meant that we sometimes talk through our body, not only through our mouth."

Max's fists unfurled as his glance fell from her hairline to her eyebrows, "Yes, yes, you *do* know!"

At that moment, Veronica reappeared, looming over both of them. Her long fingers were wrapped around the slender stems of two goblets of champagne, the rings on her fingers gleaming like eyes, the red fingernail polish looking glossily wet. She chuckled as she looked from one to the other.

IMAGES OF SANTA MUERTE

If Luisa were not a tall big-boned woman, she would have been afraid walking down the dark alleyway in Tepito, a slum in Mexico City. It was good her hair was black, her skin a light brown and that she spoke Spanish. It wasn't the melodious Spanish of Mexico. It was the hectic version from Puerto Rico.

At the end of the alley stood the Chapel of Santa Muerte. Luisa's assignment was to do a story on Saint Death for a small New York journal. The chapel offered a special service for her on the first day of every month; Luisa chose January 1. She wanted to avoid the excesses of December 31 with her friends back in Manhattan. She was surprised that at 35 her liver was still holding up.

The front desk at her three-star hotel warned her that Tepito was only a maze of littered streets full of beggars, cripples, pickpockets and gun-wielding drug traffickers. She was told that the worshippers of Santa Muerte were renegade Catholics who prayed for protection while harming others—"Santa Muerte is no saint, only the accomplice of criminals!" Luisa merely nodded her head, mentally transforming the saint's worshippers into outcasts, abandoned by the government, disparaged by their church. "Certainly," Luisa thought, "the sweetie-pie Virgin of Guadalupe, Mexico's darling, did not empathize with them!"

Luisa bowed her head as she entered through the ancient wooden door into the smoke-filled chapel. She marveled at the glitter, the abundance of gold-framed paintings. Stepping up close to the portraits she saw bejeweled anthropomorphic creatures, half-animal, half-human, and she saw hooded grinning skeletons. They were reflected over and over again by ornate mirrors illuminated by tall candles in gold holders. Beyond stood a life-size statue of Santa Muerte, skull-faced, fleshed-out hands, sequined gown, feathered boa. She was surrounded by offerings of chocolate, whiskey, cigars and jewelry. Mariachi music played in the background as people began to line up to step up close to their saint to touch her, to kiss her. These fervent followers prayed audibly for food, money, love, sex, miracles, hope and above all they prayed for salvation, for a rescue from all the evil within and without.

As the hour of twelve noon approached, more and more people crowded together not minding the physical contact, the blending of aromas of sweat, fragrant oils, remnants of food, smoke, but nowhere was there a smell of filth, of decay. Luisa was swept along towards the statue in a circular surge going towards the saint and away from her. She stood transfixed in front of the smiling idol as people behind her muttered, "Hable, hable!" Que deseas?" Speak! What do you wish for?

Without thinking Luisa lifted one hand as if it held a jigger glass and made a toast, while with the other hand she patted, then flicked her upper dentures, opening her mouth a little so that she had a grin of her own. Though she said nothing, a few women nearby laughed as if they guessed what Luisa was silently saying. They thought she was rebelliously mocking the man, the men who had hurt her.

In the end the energetic surge deposited her back at the front door and out into the alley. Feeling faint she leaned against a scabrous wall. Soon she sensed a tall presence by her side, a strong hand holding her up by one elbow.

When she was able to stand straight, to turn her head, she saw a brown man with a lopsided tangled afro, a melancholic flare in his large brown eyes.

"Hello, my name is Nicholas but call me Nico. Are you okay?" he asked removing his hand from her arm.

"I'm fine, just a little dizzy for the moment, thank you." Then extending her hand she added, "I'm Luisa."

But as she began to walk she swayed a little. Nico quickly grabbed her by the arm again, "You better let me get you a taxi; it's quite far off and this is no place for a stranger!"

"Is it that obvious I'm a stranger?" she asked brushing his hand away brusquely, noticing that his Spanish was not Mexican; she thought it had a tinge of a Portuguese accent—maybe he was from Brazil.

Nico laughed, "Yes it's very obvious and you're not as tough as you think you are!"

She looked at him more closely—he had a boyish smile and long curly eyelashes; he was younger than she'd thought, maybe only 21 or so. "You must be a stranger too—your accent, your rough clothes they're like a disguise."

Nico laughed again, this time even louder, "I guess that's why we recognized each other; we don't belong!"

Beyond the alley there was an area that resembled a plaza except that there were no trees, grass, or flowers; it was lined by vendors on all four sides selling machinery, household appliances, hunks of raw meat in all shapes and colors as if coming from esoteric creatures like snakes, lizards, wild birds and even what looked like giant spiders, locusts. Though no one was looking at her Luisa had the sensation that she was being watched, judged, that something was expected of her. Moving away from Nico she blurted out as if he'd asked her a question, "I'm a journalist; I'm always on the hunt for a story, odd, even weird stories. That's why I went to see Santa Muerte."

"What a coincidence! I'm always on the hunt too; I track pantheras, jaguars, down south!"

Luisa stopped walking. She was both fascinated and appalled by the killing of animals of such power and beauty.

"Hold on," he began understanding her expression, "I track them, running after them with a pack of dogs so they can be collared, you know, with a radio so they can be studied!" After short pause he continued, "By the way, we have to walk further than I'd thought to get you a safe taxi; I don't trust the ones around here."

"Thank you," Luisa answered softly, "I really appreciate your concern, you're very gallant in addition to obviously being a good athlete!"

Luisa had always loved the legs on runners, the mixture of slenderness and prominent muscles. She herself had strong legs but without the fine sculpting. She often dreamt of running—wild horses on beaches, soldiers in vast battlefields, lonely cross-country runners, Indians leaping from cliff-to-cliff, children racing from room-to-room screeching with terror and glee, herself running in the night from the hounds of heaven or hell.

"Hey," Nico began, returning to guiding her by the elbow, "I know this is awfully sudden, but what the hell, I'm known to be impulsive, why don't you join us on our next hunt? We've all been complaining that no one writes about us!"

"Oh my, I don't know what to say; I don't really know you and who's 'we'?" Luisa stopped walking, turning to look at Nico.

"We're scientists and we're runners like me. Let me give you some names and numbers and you can check us out back at your hotel."

Later that afternoon Luisa found out that Nicolas Matoso and his team worked for a conservation organization committed to studying and saving endangered wildlife. In actuality she'd almost said "yes" from the very beginning; in her youth she certainly would have, but that was before she promised herself to think before she jumped. She knew she would be able to sell an article on tracking jaguars and all she had to do to be free was to send off her piece on the Chapel of Santa Muerte. "That reminds me," she thought, "I must remember to ask Nico what he was doing in the "Chapel!"

• • •

The next day Nico and Luisa were in the Calakmul Biosphere Reserve in la Selva Maya, a vast expanse of tropical forest stretching through southeastern Mexico and parts of Guatemala and Belize. Their base was an old Mexican farm, a complex of wooden structures where running water and electricity had been recently installed early in the year 2000.

As their Jeep approached the farm Luisa could hear the relentless barking of dogs. By the time they climbed out of the vehicle the baying was deafening.

"Aye Nico, you're back just in time," Cesar shouted running to embrace the younger man who towered over him, "We've finally gotten a whiff of el tigre—wait till you see the claw marks he left on that tree out there!" and he pointed to the edge of the clearing. "We've got to get going as soon as possible; the dogs are more than ready!" He smiled at Luisa as if it were completely natural that a woman accompanied Nico.

Luisa was introduced to everyone as a bilingual journalist who would help get their project on the map both in Mexico and the U.S. She was examined carefully; she was admired for her self-confidence, independence, stature and physique; she could have been Nico's older sister.

After she'd quickly changed into boots, thick cotton trousers and tunic she was warned of possible dangers, sharp jagged limestone underfoot, vines with dagger-like thorns, web-like branches as well as poisonous snakes and insects.

The venture was like a parade of sorts—the six dogs in the lead, then Nicholas, afterwards came Cesar, the dog manager, along with Octavio, the field biologist with his tranquilizing dart. Luisa was expected to pull up the rear but she ended up able to keep up with Cesar and Octavio. All that climbing up and down the Corozai Mountains of Puerto Rico, not on the road but through the rainforest, was paying off. The difference was that in her youth she hadn't been moving towards anything or anywhere; she'd merely been running away from her father and her older brothers. However, one time she'd fallen off a ledge resulting in the loss of all her upper teeth; she had always blamed her family.

Nico was out of sight almost immediately as he streaked after the clamorous dogs who smelled out the path of the jaguar. The rest of the group followed the sound of the hounds.

After a few hours of stumbles, bruises, itchy bites and waterfalls of perspiration they all ended up together in a small clearing under a giant ancient tree. The jaguar had taken refuge in its thick upper branches; he was elegantly still, crouched, snarling with a deep resonance. The dogs appeared so small, so mobile, yelping as if in pain. Eventually Cesar muzzled them so that the jaguar could calm down in preparation for being sedated. Though of course the Beauty of the Beast didn't know it, they had to be careful not to harm him. He could suffer a massive heart attack or he could become ferocious attacking the dogs or one of them before the dart could be shot into his rump.

Once el tigre was quietly lying on his side on the brambly ground, Luisa knelt down close to him. She looked at him with a worshipper's awe, 8 feet long, of course counting the length of his tail, 180 pounds to maybe 200, the weight of a healthy tall hefty muscular human. His mouth was open revealing fangs the size of a man s little finger; his coat, his cloak was made up of shiny black spots, circles and swirls spread over his goldenness.

As the men rested nearby drinking water and smoking Cuban cigars, she stroked the panthera's face—what a marvel of massive bones housing so many skills, energies, hungers, pleasures, fears. It was no wonder the Aztecs and the Maya had attempted to emulate him in ceremonies, to recreate him in their art, always admiring his elusiveness, his individualistic solitary ways. As if in prayer, her lips barely moving, Luisa murmured, "You are so perfect, so accepting of life and death. You have no need to protect yourself with ceremonies, with pyramids, with envy, hatred and warfare."

Nico sauntered over to her side. He knelt down,

immediately stroking the jaguar's long corded spine, "Bellîsimo, no?"

"Yes, yet what a capacity for deadliness," she whispered, still mesmerized.

"But he's not deadly on purpose," Nico countered with some indignation.

Luisa continued, "Should it matter whether on purpose or not?"

"Of course, it makes all the difference," Nico argued, "It's the difference between premeditated crimes and crimes of passion, don't you see?"

Luisa sighed, "But the result is the same—mutilation, suffering, death."

"But that's part of life, Nico continued, "a vine can do it, a hole in the ground, a pool of water, lightning."

Touching Nico's shoulder, looking straight into his eyes Luisa asked, "Have you ever committed such a crime, you know, what's called manslaughter—have you ever slaughtered inadvertently?"

Nico's face became very still, "Perhaps, and you?"

"Perhaps," Luisa answered, almost inaudibly.

They looked at each other knowingly, guardedly, not daring to ask any more questions. In any case Cesar and Octavio were walking over to them. It was time for all of them to lift the jaguar, to move him to a different place near the thickets so that when he woke up he could quickly make his escape. Cesar, Octavio and the dogs hid quite far away, out of sight; Luisa and Nico stayed close by to watch the awakening.

El tigre opened his eyes with a start, immediately

attempting to get up, not understanding why he was so wobbly. His legs wouldn't straighten all the way leaving him in a crouching, squatting position, his back legs splayed out to the side. He wagged his head from side-to-side aware of something alien around his neck. Eventually as if in slow motion he crept away, skulked away into the thick bushes as if embarrassed, turning his head back to look in Luisa's and Nico's direction, his eyes baleful, suspicious, as if he knew they were the reason for his loss of dignity.

The dogs, Cesar and Octavio walked rapidly back to the base, happy with their success, eager to drink their cervezas; even the dogs enjoyed beer. Luisa and Nico hiked back slowly, distractedly, looking at each other warily, skulking a little like the jaguar, embarrassed, exposed. Finally Luisa asked, "Why did you go to the Chapel of Santa Muerte?"

"I was curious about la Santa," Nico was taken aback.

"But what was it about her that made you seek her out?" Luisa persisted.

"I wanted a word with her, that's all," Nico was becoming defensive.

"May I ask about what?" Luisa asked stumbling a little, not watching where she was stepping.

"Something personal."

Taking him by the arm, hanging on to it slightly, Luisa asked, "If I tell you something of what I was thinking when I saw Santa Muerte will you tell me something in return?"

"Yes," he answered slowing his pace.

Luisa sighed, wondering why she was doing what she was doing; she felt compelled; it was the same as the compulsion she sometimes had to "flash" her bare breasts at parties when she'd been drinking or the compulsion to touch someone's behind, male or female, not really wanting anything, especially not sex. She began, "When I looked up at Santa Muerte's smile I was thinking that she was such an imposter, such a fraud, pretending to be so comfortable with her losing face, comfortable having her face worn down to rock bottom or should I say worn down to the bone, when what she really wanted was to never die!"

"What does that have to do with you? No one really wants to die, not really," he was becoming impatient.

"What I'm getting at in my own way," Luisa began irritably, "is that I'm really the walking dead having killed myself long ago so as not to be possessed by my father and brothers."

"My God, how awful—" Nico muttered.

"Yes, I murdered myself in order not to be a slave to their needs, their wants, their passions!"

Nico stopped to face her, patting her shoulders, "Forgive me but you look very alive to me! How are you dead?"

Luisa continued walking, "I can't love anymore, well maybe in a one night sort of way, but not in a higher form. I can tell you this because I'm so much older than you and most likely after this project, after my story is written we won't see each other again. My stories are all that matters to me!"

Nico shrugged his shoulders defiantly, "So much the better because I've actually killed someone; I was asking Santa Muerte whether or not to give myself up to the law."

"May I ask you for details?" Luisa queried.

"No," Nico exclaimed. Then wavering he said, "Maybe—." He began to walk faster, crunching down hard on brambles, on rocks, shoving vines, branches aside with great force, "I became an orphan early on; I *wanted* to be an orphan; I wanted to be free! I killed my parents when I was a boy. Everyone said it was an accident but I set the fire on purpose!"

Silence. Neither spoke for many minutes.

"You're shocked?" Nico finally asked angrily.

"Yes, yes of course, but look at what you're doing now to conserve, to preserve life!" she protested.

"You don't think I'm a monster?" he asked.

"No, do you think *I* am? After all I truly have killed myself—I can't love or be loved, I can't bear children, I can only hunt for my stories to make a living, if you can call it that!"

"No," Nico murmured, what you've done is not monstrous, it's all in your imagination."

Silence again. Then Nico laughed, "Well, if we're not monsters, if el tigre is not a monster, then who is?"

Luisa laughed, "We all are and yet we're not!" She paused for a second. "I see it now! That's what Santa Muerte is telling us!"

"What do you mean? What *is* she telling us?" Nico queried.

"She's telling us that we're afraid to dream, we're afraid to wake up, we're all afraid to live. So, what do we do? We create nightmares, beautiful extravagant nightmares like herself!"

THE EYES OF MEDUSA

Though she was no longer a practicing psychotherapist, Joanna had consented to see Tierka on a temporary basis. Then she agreed to visit her in her home because Tierka insisted she must show her something. From the beginning she'd found the young woman extremely compelling–tall, willowy, so supple she seemed to waft when she moved, her long blond curls floating around her head, circling her piercing blue eyes. Though she was from Finland she reminded Joanna of some of the blue-eyed nomads from the Sahara Desert.

Joanna enjoyed her walk to Tierka's house in Greenwich Village, up and down cobblestone lanes, lined by old quaint homes, vines growing up the walls, flowerpots hanging from window ledges. One of the oldest houses was the one she sought; the door was slightly ajar. Nevertheless she tried the knocker, a large rusty lion's head—the sound that resulted was only a dull thud. She walked in slowly expecting Tierka to meet her, but no one appeared. The back of the house was so close to the front that the tree in the patio loomed out at her through the open back door. To the left of the entranceway was a tiny office crammed with a desk, file cabinets and stacks of foreign language journals. As she approached the desk she saw large handwriting on a pad of yellow-lined paper—perhaps a note left for her to read.

> Listen Sea, stand still for a moment so that my words may ring out over your blue and green vastness. I feel humble in your majestic presence. I am proud to behold you but I cannot compete with your eloquence. I tremble. My eyes fill with tears, but I must speak, whether you listen or not.
>
> Oh Sea, how is it you are constantly strong, unendingly sparkling? Are you never stayed by the fear that one day you may fail and all your exuberance will be of no avail?
>
> Come Sea, answer me, tell me how to alleviate my incertitude and inertia.
>
> You do not answer, do you? I remain as I was when I came to you. I can but envy you. I can but dream and observe. How vapid to merely be an onlooker. But it is my fate and will be my nemesis, my doom, unless—

Joanna sighed. Yes, this revealed both how young Tierka was and also how ancient—she was both the Sea and the beholder, the admirer and the hater. Joanna trembled a little; it was what she had sensed in their few sessions; it was something she saw lurking behind Tierka's cold blue eyes. But it wasn't clear what had led to her bitterness. Her disappointments were not unusual—not enough love, support, appreciation from employers, lovers, friends; not enough understanding of her foreignness, her isolation. During one session she'd surprised Joanna by saying in a dramatic voice, "No one has ever come close to lifting the veil that covers me, but then, perhaps to unveil me, to truly see me, is to die."

Joanna realized she'd only briefly glanced at Tierka during their sessions—for such a beautiful graceful creature she had a couple of extremely unbecoming habits; now and then she picked her teeth with a miniature pocketknife without covering her mouth and she gnawed at the torn off leaves of one of Joanna's office plants. She wondered if these habits were purposeful like the spines of a porcupine to keep others at a distance.

The room next to the small office was a kitchen, the only other room on the floor. When she noticed that the kitchen had no aromas, no garbage, not even the humming sound of the refrigerator her curiosity was further aroused. The tree in the patio was old with a long outstretched limb held up on a clothesline, wrapped in white linen—an area had come unraveled—Joanna saw blackened burnt wood.

Climbing the stairs she entered a room occupying the whole second floor. The walls were lined with books, all of them covered with brown paper. Near the front windows she saw a collapsed sunken couch, the upholstery, the stuffing and an old plaid blanket all meshed together in shreds. Proceeding to the third floor, she found only two uninhabited bedrooms. Then hearing a sound back on the second floor she ran back downstairs. Tierka lay on her side on the nest-like couch, snuggled against its back, her curls half covering her face. Joanna approached her cautiously, "Tierka, are you okay? I've been looking for you."

"I'm not okay. Nothing has changed."

"I thought you wanted to show me something," Joanna murmured, moving closer to the couch.

"I wanted to show you my life as it ebbs away," Tierka brushed some of her hair away from her mouth and nose.

Joanna chuckled, bending over Tierka, "Come on, Tierka, you're a vibrant young woman, your whole life is ahead of you."

Tierka lifted her head, "Then come and lie next to me, with your back to me."

Joanna straightened up. Seeing a stepladder near the bookcase she dragged it to the side of the couch and sat down, "You know I can't do that. I shouldn't even be here, but I was worried about you."

Tierka smiled.

"Tell me, your *Ode to the Sea*, is that what you wanted to show me? No, it can't be—you could have brought it to my office. So, what is it Tierka? Try to tell me as simply, as directly as you can."

"You know I can't do that! I can't be direct."

"Try, Tierka, tell me what you need to show me."

"Come lie next to me and I'll be direct."

"Use words, Tierka," Joanna was a little stern.

"I *am* using words. I asked you to lie next to me. What do you think I'm going to do to you?" Tierka laughed, "What's wrong with what I'm asking?"

Joanna was so flustered she didn't answer right away. Then regaining her composure she asked, "What would it mean to you, my lying next to you?"

"I want to verify that you're real."

"Isn't it enough I'm here, as you requested, that I care for your well being?"

"No, it's not enough! I'm still all alone with nothing to hold onto."

"Imagine I'm next to you. What do you say? What would you want me to say?" Joanna leaned forward, perched awkwardly on the narrow step.

Tierka laughed, "You should see how silly you look, so professional, so superior! Why don't *you* try being direct? Why don't you ask yourself what you're really doing here?"

Joanna was dumbfounded. As the room slowly began to darken, she could only sigh, suddenly feeling very weary. The girl was right—she *had* been looking for something. Was it the adventure of peering within the psyche of youth? Did she need to be appreciated, admired once again? Or was she fancying herself a savior of the lost?

Her face no longer visible in the dusk, Tierka whispers hoarsely, "Now who is it who can't find words? I knew it all along. You're a fraud. It's as if you're not here, never have been, and never will be. You might as well leave."

A profound silence descended upon the room. Joanna could hardly see anything; she could only smell the moldy couch and the dusty books. Groping her way she crept downstairs and left the house.

As she walked slowly down the street, one thing was clear, she and Tierka had enacted the drama of the medusa and the snail, the drama of a tiny parasitic jellyfish living on the back of a sea slug. However, at different stages of their lives, they exchanged roles, thus each becoming both predator and prey.

THE VIPER AND THE CROCODILES

My name is Paco.

I think I am dying but strangely enough I don't know if I'm scared—often I am not aware of what I am feeling. Anyway, I've been throwing up all day long, throwing up all over my Brooks Brothers' suit—by the way, it was custom made for me because I'm shorter than the average man—only 5'4".

Finally, the vomiting stopped and I made my way to my bedroom. I felt so weak I didn't undress before lying down on my plump afghan cover, not even taking off my shoes. The nausea was gone, as well as the stomach and chest pain, but I felt an agonizing aloneness, an aloneness I had never experienced before in all of my sixty years. It had nothing to do with the fact that my beautiful, ever-loyal wife was out teaching several classes in pottery-making. The aloneness was that of a wafting piece of myself, adrift, lost, abandoned, forsaking me or being forsaken—perhaps it was my soul.

I tried to sleep but couldn't; my mind was nagging at me to remember something. It has even given me wings with which to fly back into time, to the top of a mountain in Mexico. With strong youthful legs I land in a tiny radio station, one of the first such stations in the beginning of Pan American Airways' adventure in Latin America. So long ago—1920's. I was big, important—I guided and saved lost and crippled airplanes as they flew in tumultuous weather from Miami to Mexico City. To think I sent messages to radio operators in the plane on a simple hand-operated radio. I knew the terrain intimately by having flown over it in a two-seater plane—I knew the volcanoes, the lakes, the valleys as well as I knew the geography of my body.

Sometimes I wondered how I was able to accept the primitive conditions up on my mountain. No running water, spare, dry plant life. A peon and his donkey brought me water and food everyday, from the nearest village at the bottom of my mountain. I was too hot during the day and cold, shivery at night, enjoying the warm glow of the distant volcanoes.

I'm almost embarrassed to admit that my greatest solace came from a secret friend, no, not one in my imagination as with children and their invisible playmates. My secret pleasure was derived from Tres Narices, a slithering, seductive creature who embraced me with all of her being. She was a vibrant being in lavender and brown. She was a viper who would wrap herself around my neck and shoulders, all the time pulsating, writhing as if she was listening to the beating of jungle drums. You may find it strange but I actually talked to her and I imagined her talking back to me. Let me tell you about one conversation. I asked,

"Why do I love you, a simple creature who can only coil and uncoil, a creature who stares at me with naked unadorned eyes?" She answers,

"Because I'm the only one here for you. The only one who can love a loner like myself who's forever looking for warm-bloodied prey."

"But why?" I asked, "Why can't I just be happy existing? Why not be happy with leaving my mark on a tree, a post, on a rock, like a beast?"

"Because, my little man, we have been chosen to prove that we can love and be loved."

This angered me even though I was the one imagining her words, so I retorted,

"What would you know about love, you three-nosed freak?"

She wagged her tongue at me, her way of laughing, "You'd be surprised. I was the one who was present at Earth's first love affair, the one between Adam and Eve. I was the one who intertwined them with a rope of leaves while offering them the world in the form of an apple.

"Forget all that; why do we have to prove we can love and be loved?" I asked,

"Because we are freaks, because we don't belong anywhere, to any group, we can't be classified because we are not anything more than what we are," she retorted before continuing, "Stop thinking, just live your life."

Then I became aware I was lying on my afghan still wearing my soiled Brooks Brothers suit. Had I lived a life, being loved, loving another? I married a Maya-Mexican woman, given her a good life, had three daughters, educated them to cherish a life free of all doctrines, concepts of religion, morality, identifications. Did I do wrong? Did I teach them to be freaks like myself, thus leading to my feeling more isolated and alone than ever? After all, loners cannot truly connect with other loners. But in any case, the painful aloneness I feel has nothing to do with my family. It's something deeper, more primeval.

I knew I had to explore further, somehow I sensed time was waiting. I remembered another radio station, this time on the island of Cozumel, near Mexico. The station consisted of a shack on stilts at one end of the island and a small village at the other end. In between was an impassible strip of land full of crevices where waves clamored dragging everything in its path back into the sea, including mango roots that had allowed themselves to become loose. Food and water were delivered every day by a motor launch from the village. I missed my viper Tres Narices, on the island all I had for company was a group of crocodiles that lived under my cabin. They weren't graceful, elegant, groaning and grunting, slapping the silky sand with their clumsy tails. I'd heard that the previous radio operator's pet dogs had all been snatched away, right under his nose, never to return. I guessed the crocs had claimed them as a form of rent, after all they were the landlords. I was warned not to fall outside, never to be injured, helpless. I suppose the beasts would then be certain they were being presented with a special tribute, a small but sturdy warm-bloodied morsel.

One day an executive from United Fruit Company

came to visit, bringing German beer and American steaks. He was so very inquisitive.

"Aren't you lonely, here by yourself, still under thirty, unmarried, no girlfriends?"

"Sure, sometimes, but I've had many encounters up to now," I responded not sharing my memories with him—riding the rails all over the United States, being given shelter by lonely women and by adventurous young girls. Also there was nothing that compared with being a merchant seaman, visiting every exciting harbor in the world with their women of all colors and sizes.

My guest continued, "But why can't you settle down to enjoy one beautiful woman, one warm receptive body for a change?"

"Why should I?"

"It's not natural, your having only yourself as your main suitor!" Malcolm laughed raucously making an obscene gesture with one hand around his crotch.

I was incensed, "What difference does it make if there's no real love, adoration, connectiveness with the other—it would still be a waste of the seed of life whether it is spilt upon the ground or spilt inside an alien body?"

"Paco, you speak so strangely; you've truly been alone too long. Listen, I know a pretty young Mexican woman who needs work as a housekeeper/cook. Who knows, she may even take a liking to you, what do you say?"

"I don't know, Mal, I'm really timid."

"Yes, but she's also shy, poor, inexperienced, you'd have the upper hand."

Despite myself, something began to glow within me,

as Malcolm chuckled, slapping his knees and stamping upon the wooden planks of the hut with his heavy boots, totally unaware that the animals beneath were slapping each others' tails in concordance, grinning widely, showing their jagged teeth.

The very next day the woman arrived in the launch. I'd already seen her from afar, long masses of hair turning somersaults in the wind. She was as tiny, as slender as a child. Once arriving she hardly spoke to me, only telling me she was called Luna. Her few possessions were wrapped up in a bright silk shawl. She seemed interested only in the location of my clean-up supplies and of her room. Using sign language, indicating she needed a nap she disappeared into her room, loudly locking her door, refusing to understand my Spanish; it was fluent but heavily accented.

I was dismayed. Now, besides still being alone I was saddled with a hostile force disturbing my peace of home. But that night as I laid sleepless listening to the low roaring of the crocodiles, the unexpected happened. Luna crept into my room, into my narrow cot, naked, her dark hair hanging over her breasts.

"*Mi amorcito*, my little love," she began caressing my head with its sparse tufts of baby hair. It was as if she knew how ashamed I was of being almost bald since the age of five when I was lured away from my beloved foster mother to go to live with my birth mother—the loss was manifested by my head of hair being shed, never to return except in random wisps. Luna's affection towards my humble scalp made me fall in love with her. I made love to her over and over again that night. By morning Luna looked at me not only with affection but with great respect. For the first time in my life I felt tall, gallant, like a true "*caballero*." We were happy for many months. Then came a warning from Miami that a monster hurricane was coming to the Caribbean—"Leave post immediately. Danger."

If I had been alone I would have stayed to be of help to all who needed to communicate—I'd heard that a tidal wave had overrun a college in Belize, a school full of enthusiastic young aspiring souls. But not being alone, Luna and I departed for the mainland, to the town of Chetumal. In the only hotel available, everyone gawked at me, the *gringo* and the young brown girl. One day Malcolm took me to one side, "What's the matter with you, she's a great lay but why are you treating her like a wife, dining with her in public. I didn't think I had to spell it out—she's only a cheap whore."

I knocked him to the floor with one blow to his long lantern jaw. But this did not assuage my agony—back in our room I slapped my beloved Luna, sobbing and yelling at the same time, "You've played me for a fool, an *idiota*. When were you going to move in for the kill, for the payoff?"

"You're so wrong, I like you; you're different from other men; you're good, kind, needy, even beautifully innocent. I want nothing from you but your '*fuerza de la vida*,' your life force, your passion."

But I was already blind, deaf, a mute creature. I grabbed a few of my belongings and I left the room, the hotel, the town and I returned to my radio station, to the crowd of snuggling, snoring crocodiles as the wind began to howl and the waves drew themselves up like a myriad cobras.

I squirmed with pain as I lay on my bed in Mexico City. I had truly loved Luna, yet I had forsaken her. Had this led to my now feeling that terrible aloneness; had I left my soul with her without being aware of it all these years? As my eyes began to close perhaps for the last time, as I smelled the stink of vomit on my Brooks Brothers suit, I knew I would never know the answer. I was only a tiny bald man sitting on a crocodile with a lavender-brown viper around my neck.

TRICKSTERS

Looking crisp in his maroon tuxedo jacket, the bartender placed a square white handkerchief with knots at each corner on top of a large lemon; chuckling he sent it rolling down the counter. Not knowing how far the albino headless toad would be able to toddle, I quickly picked up my martini goblet. However, the little specter came to a stop nearby, in front of my neighbor, a woman who merely sighed deeply, continuing to smoke her cigarette, her luxurious fur coat draped thickly around the back and sides of her stool, the cloud of smoke and furry hide both occluding and expanding her presence.

Not long before, without turning to look at me she had sighed that same sigh of disdain as I had scraped my high stool around on the tile floor to facilitate my climbing up on it. I smiled at the boyish-looking bartender as he sheepishly retrieved his toy; I noticed at the same time that the woman was beautifully made-up, thick long lashes, perfectly blended tones of rose upon her cheeks, outlined red lips which left no marks upon the rim of her whiskey glass. As I continued to glance at her surreptitiously, I noticed what I hadn't before, that her eye was half-hooded by tired flesh and tiny lines radiated from the corners of her eye and lips; at least she must have laughed a great deal at some time in her life. She was definitely younger than I since my flesh had already left its safe anchoring to bone and had gone its own way.

"What are you thinking about?" I almost ask the woman, being used to posing that question to the many who had been next to me, throughout my long life. But instead I chuckle to myself as the woman curtly ordered another scotch on the rocks, as if in response to my unasked question, as if to say, "I'm thinking how unbearably thirsty I still am and how I wish someone else were seated by my side!" Drinking it down as if it were water she put down a twenty dollar bill, gathered up her fur coat into a large ball as if it were a baby bear and hurriedly left.

As I ordered another martini straight up, dry, this time with a twist instead of olives, a rich aroma permeated the atmosphere as someone lithely slipped onto the stool the woman had left; it was a mixture of fragrant oils with an underlying scent of lemon verbena. I sensed a tall form next to me, a blondness that almost shone like a light; I heard the rustle of a silk-lined jacket, the clink of cufflinks upon the edge of the counter, a male voice ordering champagne. I was transfixed not wanting to break the spell by turning to look at him. Gradually, his aroma revealed subtler aspects, the unmistakable essence of a man, a man who had just had sex, or was I imagining it? I turned myself around to look at him but I made the mistake of not first preparing my balance; as I wobbled a little atop my stool, he turned in my direction. I almost fainted. Before me was a vision of grandeur: waves of thick golden hair sweeping backwards, large sparkling blue eyes, glowing skin, dimples that had grown into the shape of crescent moons. He was not close, also not far away, but yet for an instant, unbeknownst to him, my eyes held him, possessed him, as I recaptured the intoxicating allure of youth and beauty. As he returned to his drink I blurted out, "Oh my God! You're the most handsome man I've ever seen!"

Once again the man turned to look at me, this time more fully, his eyes luminous but distant, an ironic smile forming on one side of his lips. Was it mocking or merely weary?

"I'm sorry," I stammered, "I didn't expect to see you, I mean someone like you!"

The man laughed with his eyes almost closed as if blinded by his own radiance. After taking a long gulp of his drink, he sighed deeply looking at his watch. I chuckled to myself, content to be where I was, in my own space, happy to have had a glorious moment, relieved to have left it behind.

EL PÍCARO, THE ROGUE GENTLEMAN

The door to the room across from the nurses' station was partially ajar. It was barely after dinnertime but there was no light coming from within. The three main nurses kept asking themselves why they were tip-toeing around whispering to each other. Even though they worked on a special floor for severely ill patients with chronic ailments they had never behaved like this before, that is until El Pícaro had moved in across from them. The relatives that had recently escorted him to his room in his wheelchair with one foot propped up called him just "Pico." Before leaving, never to be seen again, these family members told the nurses that Pico deserved what had happened to him, being bitten by a poisonous snake on Isla de Culebras, Island of Serpents, off the eastern mainland of Puerto Rico. They recounted with righteous indignation how Pico had been partying on heavy drugs with sailors from a nearby naval base before getting attacked by the serpent. Believing him to be dead the frightened sailors had abandoned him. Upon awakening, Pico had slithered on his belly seeking help. After a short stay in a Naval Hospital his family in San Juan shipped him to family in New York where he eventually ended up where he was now in a Manhattan hospital on a specially endowed floor with extra shiny floors, fresh flowers in the lounges, plushly-cushioned easy-chairs in all the rooms, and with especially trained dedicated nurses who worked longer shifts than usual, alternating between all-day and all-night shifts.

Pico endeared himself to the three nurses by enthusiastically asking each of them what their name was and from where they had come—Nancy, the head-nurse, half-Chinese living in the Bronx, a specialist in infectious diseases; Aurelia, who had originated from the same spot as Pico had in Puerto Rico, the Mountains of Corozai; the third nurse Latisha was still a resident nurse. She admired Pico's neatness, his cleanliness, his use of aromatic oils procured from the cleaning woman. He insisted on helping Latisha make his bed hopping around on one leg like a heron or a crane.

Then, looking like an elegant owl with his deeply-set black eyes, his aquiline nose, brushed back black hair, a fringe of whiskers on his jaw line he would regale the three nurses with stories of his rainforest up near the clouds, in the bamboo jungle of the mountains of Corozai. He'd tell them of frogs that looked like dragons, bats that walked upright like humans, wild dogs resembling werewolves, dancing adders and goats that traveled alone, not as part of a herd.

As time went on and Pico's foot refused to heal despite strong antibiotics, it was decided he needed surgery to cut out the afflicted flesh to try to prevent blood poisoning. As Nancy washed and disinfected his foot, Pico told her that he knew what his malady meant in a larger sense.

"Don't do this to yourself!" Nancy pleaded, "You got bitten, it was neglected, it got infected—that's that!"

But Pico persisted, "I know this may sound strange but my foot is what holds me up, my foundation, the pedestal from which I've fallen. I'm being punished for being careless, loose, footloose."

Gently massaging the lean atrophied legs Nancy continued, "Sounds good but it's all nonsense! You've been punished enough with what you went through on that island all by yourself! You must have been in terrible pain and you must have been so frightened!"

Wincing, the slightest touch on his skin bringing on ripples of pain throughout his body, Pico murmured, "Yes, I wanted to die. If I'd had a knife I would have chopped off my foot and then I would have shoved the blade into my heart. What kept me going was knowing that I needed to suffer."

"No one needs to suffer like that! It happens enough with just plain living!" Nancy exclaimed.

As they looked at his brick-red clenched foot, toes tangled, twisted downwards as if they'd been forcefully bound as was done to Chinese girls of long ago, Nancy couldn't see the charm, the beauty that had been seen in the resulting vulnerability, the helplessness. She'd never seen any good reason for any form of human suffering.

The day of the foot surgery finally arrived. Pico fought against the anesthetic, pushing his eyelids open but soon the doctors in blue disappeared as did the bright overhead lights. A gigantic tractor looking like a tank was coming towards him, slowly at first, then faster and faster. He slumped down upon the furrowed earth. He was ploughed under like a giant seed.

The next thing he knew was being wheeled around, strapped down. Was he in a baby carriage? The lights were a whirling blue and orange. "Where am I?" he heard himself asking in a croaky voice.

"Delivery Room."

Did he hear right? "No, Recovery Room."

Opening his eyes, Pico tried lifting his head to no avail but he kept trying. Eventually he was able to rise up a little, to look downwards. He saw a large bundle cradled in a sling. It swayed a little, demanding attention. His whole body writhed in response. Was he re-created? Was he being given another chance?

Pico recovered enough to wander the halls of the floor using a cane—tall, erect but getting thinner and thinner everyday, his gauntness giving him the look of a walking Giacometti statue. Pico had sewn together several hospital gowns making a flowing cape tied together on his shoulders. The other patients were drawn to his priestly, ethereal appearance, to his mysterious words, to his gliding winged movements. Every night many gathered by flashlight in his room. One night Pico began humming an old song from his rainforest. Everyone joined in with him, their voices reaching such high notes that the three nurses stopped what they were doing, putting a hand on their hearts as if they were in agony. To Aurelia the sound was like the owl's nocturnal call heralding the message that a life was about to end.

Tommy, who had only one eye, asked, "What can we do to save our souls, to save them from our fucking bodies?"

"Just keep on humming," Pico answered. "Let your voice vibrate throughout all of you, breaking down all your walls and then you'll know."

"What is Pico doing?" Nancy asked her co-workers as she brought out the drug tray and began counting out pills into tiny plastic containers.

"Who knows!" Aurelia whispered. "I hear only a word here and there, sometimes in English, sometimes in Spanish."

What words?" Nancy asked.

"'Bad,' 'good,' words like that."

"Poor Pico," said Nancy, sniffling a little, "He doesn't have long, you know. The surgery hasn't helped. It was probably too late even when he was brought here to us. I told him he should write his life story. Imagine, youngest of eighteen kids, breastfed by an older sister who had just had a baby of her own, growing up wild, living in caves with other runaways, hustling on the beaches in San Juan, but always reading whatever books he could get his hands on.

• • •

"I still don't know what to do to make things right," moaned Tommy and many of the men and women gathered in Pico's room nodded in agreement. Some were missing limbs, were blind, some had cancerous lesions, all were ravaged.

Pico paced up and down, dragging his foot behind him, his face, arms and hands looking a bilious yellow in the reflected light.

"Make peace with everyone you've wronged!" Face them in person or in your imagination. Accept their dirty looks, their rejecting of you, their accusations. Feel their hurt, their anger."

All the patients watched, waited, curious about the people Pico would beckon to come to see him for the cleansing of his spirit. In their minds they would consist of those from whom he'd stolen money, checks, jewelry, coin collections; the youngsters he'd seduced; as well as the ones he'd beaten and maimed in street fights. But no one appeared. Not one person from the outside came to see him. In the meantime, Pico's life slowly seeped out, his energy ebbing, leaving him lying quietly in his bed.

One night, very late, after midnight, the three nurses left their station and came to see Pico.

"Are you okay? Would you like some extra painkillers?" Nancy asked.

"No," Pico answered.

"Do you want me to tell you some news from Corozai?" Aurelia asked, "I've just had a phone call from my grandmother about the recent hurricane."

"It's okay," Pico mumbled, "I know all my animals are on the run looking for shelter from our rampaging Mother Nature."

"Can I give you a nice warm sponge bath with that lavender soap you love?" Latisha whispered, bending over, almost touching his ear with her lips, not minding the aroma that was enclosing Pico in its suffocating grip, an aroma that foretold the fate of all flesh. Just as everyone's life is a river that leads to the sea of death (as a great Spanish poet once wrote), so everyone's body is a stepping-stone to the earth's rocky core.

"Later, perhaps," Pico murmured, smiling his dazzling sensual smile, so full of mischief, the smile that had lead to his being called El Pícaro, the Rogue.

Nancy was on the verge of tears, "But what can we do for you?" "We want to do something! Tell us, what can we do?"

"Forgive me—"

"For what? You've done nothing bad to us!"

Attempting to raise his voice, Pico answered, "My great sin is that I've never been able to say, I haven't been able to say, to ask for what I really wanted from everyone."

"What is it you wanted, what you think you wanted?" Nancy implored.

"I don't know! That's just it, I don't know!" El Pícaro blurted, sighing deeply, a wail becoming stifled in his throat. "I have no footprints. I never had any footprints. I never had any footprints of my own."

TURNING AWAY

"No, no *puedo,* (I can't)," the Panamanian health aide Tomas said when I asked if he could stay the night to help me care for Eliseo who'd taken a turn for the worse. Though he had lost sixty pounds in the three months he'd been seriously ill, he was still big. In addition he was stiff, balky, disoriented, the toxins from his failing liver going to his brain, the end result of a massive bacterial attack after an accidental injury to his foot. We already knew there was no hope for survival. Eliseo had even asked me not to make a romantic thing out of his dying.

I had thought I could handle it all. I had promised him he could stay in my apartment till the end. I had even refused nightcare when the health agency had inquired about my needs. But suddenly, standing there, high up in what I called my tree house, surrounded by large windows, looking out towards roof gardens and city lights, waves of nausea descended upon me, rolling me around, splashing my whole being with a cold sweat, turning my muscles into measly sponges. Lamely, perhaps beseechingly, I asked Tomas if he could at least help me wheel Eliseo to St. Vincent's Hospital, about twenty minutes away by foot. "*Si, por supuesto! Como no*!" (Yes, of course! Why not?)

Oh my God, what was I doing? I knew what they would do to him in the Emergency Room. They had to. It was their job to keep him going, keep him alive. They would draw vials and vials of blood, roughly, quickly puncturing him with their needles, not having the time to look for the delicate butterfly needle used for difficult wandering veins; they might plunk an oxygen mask on his face, connect him to an intravenous contraption to keep him hydrated, hook a catheter into his penis, maybe put a feeding tube down his throat for his medications and fluid nutrition since he'd most likely refuse to take anything on his own. He would fight them off as if they were up to no good the way he'd resisted most of his seventeen older siblings as he was growing up, the way he'd resisted his brutal father who fancied himself a grand Spanish landowner. The only procedure he would not fight off was the injection of morphine. Only by promising him an extra pain pill had I stopped him many times from staggering out of my front door in his underwear convinced it was time for us to leave together for far-off lands. "Come on, dear woman, it's late, we must get to the airport or the plane will go without us!"

• • •

What a sight we make, three figures rushing through Greenwich Village streets under the shadows of tree branches with their shuddering leaves, a tall cadaverous huddled man strapped into a wheel chair, a husky dark man pushing the chair, now and then stopping to cover Eliseo with the blanket that kept sliding down and away, and myself, an older woman trying to keep up with Tomas. I zigzagged from one side of the sidewalk to the other, sometimes lagging behind, my mouth open, panting. We were a trinity from hell.

As the hospital attendants rushed Eliseo to a curtained-off cubicle to do what they must, I was ushered to a desk where a nurse was preparing to ask me questions so she could complete her forms, despite the fact that Eliseo's records were already on file.

Eventually I'm escorted to his side. He's very still, strapped down. I'm told he'll be admitted, that not only could I leave but that I must. I bent over to kiss him, to say goodbye, my face crinkled and wet, my hands trembling, my knees beginning to fold. Eliseo's eyes are closed, he has no mask, no oxygen mask. Sensing me, knowing my intention he turns his face violently away, deliberately, knowingly. I stretch myself, trying at least to reach his cheek. He turns further away half burying his face in the pillow, adamantly wanting to escape my touch. I end up softly caressing his earlobe with my lips. I kiss the diamond stud I'd given him on his last birthday, his fifty-fifth. The gem had beautifully accentuated his sparkling black eyes, the eyes that had always reminded me of Erroll Flynn in one of his pirate movies. Then I flee back to the waiting room, to Tomas and the empty chair that he must now wheel back to my building since there was no way I'd ever be able to get it back by myself up and down all the bumps, the steep curbs and over all the jagged cracks. But above all I'd never be able to walk all alone under the swaggering frolicking leaves.

Once home I collapsed upon my bed with all my clothes on, immediately sinking into sleep, murmuring to myself, "*Dormir, dormir como todos los olvidados*!" (To sleep like all the forgotten ones!)

Awakening with a start right before dawn I knew that for most of my life I'd been avoiding, I'd been doing everything humanly and what's worse inhumanly possible in order to prevent someone turning their face away from me.

THE BRAID

Riding on the number eleven bus from the first stop on Bethune and Greenwich Street to the upper west side is like traveling backwards in time from old age to a certain youthfulness, from crumbling townhouses and crooked cobblestones to tall apartment buildings.

Since I moved to a small condo in Greenwich Village six years ago, I have often taken the number eleven to Seventy-fifth Street and Amsterdam Avenue, and then walked one block to Broadway to my favorite Japanese Restaurant.

One rainy gray day as I trudged along, towards restaurant Bon 75, having some difficulty navigating the steep slope in front of the parking garage, I was already savoring the steamed crab dumplings, the silky salmon sashimi, and the hot sake. I wondered what little appetizer would be given to me as a gift, always in a tiny blue plate. Would it be a sesame spinach salad, lemony bits of fish, or would it be soybeans still in their pods? Looking down as always, fearful of falling on my face, I headed straight for the front door, only to realize a second later, as I looked through the large glass windows that the place was empty, totally bare—no banquette, no black tables and chairs, no spiky-leafed plants reaching for the ceiling, no paintings on the walls with calligraphic messages, no banner of a warrior hanging over the doorway leading downstairs to the cellar.

"Oh, God, no! But I never said goodbye!" I exclaimed within myself. Now I'd never be able to say goodbye to Yoshi, the waiter, the young man with one long black braid going down his back, who had paid a magnificent tribute to my friend Eliseo.

When they'd met, only a couple of years before, it was as if Yoshi and Eliseo had immediately understood each other. They had bowed a little, smiling slightly with sparkling black eyes, as they had looked directly at each other, as if Puerto Rico and Japan were one and the same. With me, Yoshi had been attentive but had never looked me straight in the eye, never smiling, though the corners of his lips had always been uplifted. Had Yoshi guessed that Eliseo and I were lovers, even though he was so much younger than I? Had he been expressing his approval, perhaps even happiness that I was no longer alone? Or had he thought Eliseo was my son, and had enjoyed the image of mother and son, reunited? Perhaps he missed his own mother; perhaps she was still in Japan. Yoshi couldn't have been in the USA too long; he barely understood English, and he spoke it with great hesitation.

How strange it had been when I told Yoshi that Eliseo had died, suddenly, from complications resulting from an accident, and I had seen tears in his eyes, as he had looked directly at me for the first time. I hadn't been able to eat anything that day and even the sake wasn't as good as usual, cooling down much too rapidly.

The following week I returned to Bon 75, not knowing it would be my last time eating there; I saw that Yoshi's long braid had disappeared. After three sakes I asked him what had happened to it, mainly using manual gestures. He had bowed a little, smiling slightly, "I cut, I cut in honor of your man."

Now, as I stood transfixed, in front of the ghost of Bon 75, I wondered if it, too, had disappeared, in honor of my Eliseo, and my love for him.

THE FLYING HORSE

Even though it had been bequeathed to me I reluctantly, guiltily picked up the Chinese bronze horse off the mantelpiece; its mane twisting and swirling in the wind, three of its hoofs off the ground as it sped through time and space. This horse had been the subject of many a session I'd had with my mentor-analyst Bianca when I had been a psychotherapist-in-training about twenty-five years ago. Becoming transfixed in the past I remember a dream I had discussed with her, one that haunted me for years, a dream from my youth of my three selves. First I'm in a kitchen stabbing someone to death, then I'm running upstairs pursued by the murderer and as I'm about to be torn to shreds by long dagger-like nails, I look out of an upstairs window and see that I am galloping off into the night on a wild horse, my long hair streaming behind me.

Bianca had listened with a gentle smile on her lips. Then brushing her long blond hair away from her face, adjusting her glasses, leaning forward on her leather chair as if about to reach for my hands, she had murmured softly, "In this dream you show that you cannot accept your feelings, your passions, that they are deserving of punishment, but unable to eradicate your emotions you decide to deny, to run." As I nodded with embarrassment feeling too imperfect to even consider being a psychotherapist, too marred to help anyone else, she had continued, "Knowing your imperfections will allow you to be of better help to others; there's nothing to be ashamed of! You know, that dream could have been mine and not only am I about twenty years older than you but I've been at this work forever!"

Still standing at the mantelpiece, still holding the flying horse, still transfixed in the past, I remember that after attending her Saturday seminars for professional psychotherapists for countless years, after many dinners together talking as friends, one day Bianca had fallen and broken her hip. Her recovery had seemed strangely long and complicated. Everyone was shocked, perplexed when she had suddenly closed down her private practice. Her seminars came to an abrupt end. I was afraid of visiting her having been told she required round-the-clock home care. But nevertheless, I did. The health aide had sat me next to Bianca opposite the television set. Bianca seemed remote, hardly acknowledging my presence, and I, not knowing what to say or do, talked on and on about her seminars, about how we all missed her, how we all looked up to her. Then surprising myself I had asked her if she remembered how timid I used to be, able to read my essays out loud but not able to easily speak extemporaneously. Bianca hadn't answered me right away but then she'd gleefully pointed to the television screen, "There you are! There you go!" Looking to see to whom she'd been pointing I see a young elegant woman making an impassioned closing argument to a jury on behalf of the defendant.

Now here I was once again in Bianca's living room, this time unable to let go of the bronze horse, yet unable to put it back on the mantelpiece. It was mine though Bianca hadn't died. She was seated behind me, once again in front of the television set. It was unbelievable but she was about to be placed in a nursing home with advanced Alzheimer's disease, her apartment already sold and about to be dismantled, her Will already read and hence her gift to me of the flying horse. That afternoon when I had first entered her home I had looked past her, looked past her still profile to the windows beyond with their view of the vast sky above the Central Park Reservoir. Now with my back to her, I look into the mirror over the mantelpiece. I'm taken aback by how old I look despite the artificial coloring of my hair, my soft features and my relatively smooth facial skin. Then surreptitiously I seek out Bianca's image within the mirror, white hair cut short, roughly, jaggedly (perhaps because she'd been pulling away, resisting), her cheeks and lips sunken as if missing her teeth, rendering her nose and chin incredibly pointed. She just sat there staring at the screen. She couldn't have been seeing much of anything for she wasn't wearing her glasses. I hated that I couldn't see her lips—they had disappeared. Suddenly a wisp of a thought passed through my mind but so rapidly that it didn't become registered.

Putting down the statue on the mantelpiece, I turn and flee down her long hallway, full of paintings and prints given to her by grateful patients. I enter Bianca's office with its immense library, now no longer neat and organized the way she'd always kept it. Now the rows of books were slanting, collapsing in every direction. Dusty stacks of paper lay on her desk. I recognize her graceful rhythmical handwriting, the light strokes in pencil quickly fading. I look at the giant leather couch where her patients had sat or lain and where mysteriously enough she herself had slept at night having no bedroom. Why had she denied herself a bed of her own? Had she been afraid of the ideas, the acts linked to a bed, rest, sleep, dreams, love, sex? A disturbing fleeting thought crosses my mind only to vanish once again. I head for the front door wanting only to pick up my horse and to leave, perhaps without even saying goodbye to Bianca, but then I hadn't even said hello. But at the door, my statue in hand, I turn my head towards the living room and unable to stop myself I rush to the still form of Bianca as she sits blindingly backlit by the distant sun. I bend down, whispering, my lips grazing her cheek, "Goodbye, dear Bianca. Thanks so much for your wisdom, for your acceptance of the flying horse within me." She turns her head looking at me with moist tender eyes, a small smile unearthing her hidden lips. The thought, the memory that had eluded me earlier became clear. I remembered that time in the taxi when I was dropping her off before going home to my family. She'd turned to me kissing me gently, firmly, fully on my lips while holding my head with warm trembling hands. I hadn't responded but neither had I resisted. She never did this again. We never discussed it. But now that I am allowing myself to remember the kiss, I realize why I had forgotten it. I think it dismays me that it was probably the most loving kiss I've ever received because it was totally without any demand, command or urgency—only a kiss expressing her love of me.

TOWARDS THE EYE OF THE ROCK

The small boat rocked up and down, to and fro on its moorings on the Bay of Ballenskelligs in southwest Ireland. Its young nervous skipper held it as tightly as possible by a rope tied around a pole on the dock. My sister Dolores who was five years younger than I and who had been a dancer in her youth, jumped nimbly upon the deck of the boat extending a hand to me, telling me to wait till the boat rose upwards to where I stood on the steps. Staccato-like as if on short wooden stilts I clambered onto the side ledge of the scabrous craft. Then backwards I descended down to a bench and then backwards again down an even steeper step to the floor of the boat, painfully stretching various tendons, ligaments surrounding my artificial knees. While seated on the middle bench untying the knotty cramps in my legs, Dolores' slanted luminous black eyes opened wide as she looked at me fully, tenderly, her delicate lips silently asking me if I should really undertake any part of our excursion to the Great Skelligs Island. It felt so good to be with her, to know her so well, all our long lives, but above all it was comforting to be known, to be knowable by her, the good, the bad, the imperfect.

"I'm fine, really I am. Look at what a glorious day it is!" I exclaimed, "Balmy winds, bright sun! Look what a deep green the waters are!"

For two hours we rolled happily around looking forward to visiting the ruins of a medieval monastery, an early Christian settlement on the top of the rock that was called Skelligs. Finally we arrive at a narrow cove where the churning waters struck out at the dock and the vertical rock rushing tempestuously into a dark cave where seconds later they battered thunderously against the back wall. As the skipper struggled to tie the frenzied boat as close to the dock as possible, the passengers jump off, one by one, some more lithely than others but none with any difficulty. I clench my teeth grinding them a little, keenly aware of my lack of springs, all having been worn away by forty-five years of rheumatoid arthritis. Dolores jumps off confidently, extending her tanned wiry hand to me, each finger jointed in a synchronous fashion, connecting to a narrow but firm wrist and forearm. Reaching for her hand with my gnarled fingers, my fused wrist and crooked elbow straining to articulate, I topple headlong onto the dock. But I do not fall, caught by the arm by Dolores who was shorter and lighter than I. After recovering my balance I baby-step sideways up a flight of cement steps hanging onto a rope banister up to a winding uphill ramp with Dolores by my side infusing me with her steady deep breathing. Then arm in arm we walk up the ramp, a pathway of jagged rocks. We look ahead of us, beyond the manmade stone wall to the precipitous cliffs lined with roosting seagulls and puffins all facing in the same direction. We look below at the restless black waters. Far away we see misty silhouetted hills.

A half hour later we arrive at the famous heavenly staircase leading to the top, six hundred steps carved right out of the rock in the middle ages. We knew without having to say that only Dolores would make the ascent. I would wait on the side of the third step. Though I was enchanted by the view of the rough waters, of all the tiny rocky islands and of the undulating hills on far-off shores looking more like mirages in the bluish golden bedazzlement of light, my mind's eye was fixed on images of steps, the steps that spanned the many stages of my life like hurdles that had had to be surmounted.

In my teens there was the staircase in our house in New York where along with my two younger sisters we danced out dramas to classical music. One day to our surprise mama came into the living room to watch us. Turning my head towards her, inwardly calling to her, "Look mommy, look! Look at me!" I lost my footing, tumbling all the way down, ending up an askew heap, not even able to pretend that the fall was part of the choreography. What was it I had been looking for in her face, in her eyes, in the pupils of her eyes? I read somewhere that the pupil of the eye in some ancient tongue is the same word as mother, the very first validating or obliterating force in our lives.

Then there were the steps in the Souk in Algiers. A group of us were descending them on our way back to our bus when it begun to rain. As everyone began to run I was left behind. I could have called out for help; I could have made my lagging presence known but I didn't, at least not out loud. Inside of myself I had shouted, "Look, look, I'm still here!" Very soon children came out of their doorways; they watched me baby-stepping downwards, a woman in her thirties, wearing pants, upper chest, throat, neck and head uncovered. The children began to giggle; then they laughed merrily pointing at me as they threw small dried fruits and nuts. Looking at their innocent inquisitive faces I felt like laughing with them, somehow knowing I would be okay; after our guide had counted heads he'd return to look for me.

Much later, one of the many hurdles that had had to be surmounted was getting home at night in a snowstorm after my car service was incapacitated. Actually this happened not so long ago, for it was only recently that I trudged home slipping and sliding by bus and by foot for fifty blocks, over a period of three hours. Bent over, crouching sometimes, I waded through icy puddles at street corners rather than climbing up and down mountains of snow left by the snowploughs as they cleared the streets for automobiles. I think I cried a little. I'm not certain if I did or didn't for slowly, slowly the storm and I had merged into a watery swirl of exhilarating energy. In a strange way we came to know each other well.

When Dolores returned from her climb of the six hundred steps we embraced; I felt as if I too had climbed up the ample warm rock, reaching the lofty haven at its pinnacle.

Once back on the rocking boat sitting quietly next to Dolores, our bodies sometimes lurching into each other, we looked back at The Great Rock of Skelligs, dark, craggy, grand; sheltering also even of toddling steps. I thought to myself that if one can say Mother Earth, why not also say Mother Rock.

MELODIES FROM THE TREETOPS

Joanna was in a beautiful place, an isolated family cabin in the mountains; she was on a veranda facing a meadow, a pine forest and distant hills. She was alone, the hosts having gone on an afternoon hike. No sounds for the moment as she let her mind go blank. No movements as she sank into a peaceful stillness. She'd had decades of experience in disappearing despite the bulkiness that had enveloped her once lithe figure.

However, the voices of the stately tall pines at the edge of the meadow would not be still; the lisping breeze within their spikiness proclaimed that in the winter of Joanna's life spring had arrived. For her it was the time when birds mate with lizards or when the essence of snakes evaporates into the air returning downwards into the hidden haunts of eagles or owls; it is the time when Chimeras are conceived. Joanna hated to admit that it was her kind of time and always had been. It was the time when no matter how at peace she was, she was exposed, revealed as a many-genomed hybrid, ungrounded, freely floating, belonging nowhere; with this identity came the hooded cloak of shame.

Joanna knew that the aim of shame is disappearance; she knew this as achieved through hiding, shape-shifting, stupefaction or denial of self. She knew how to play these tricks on her mind, spirit and even her body; she could do a virtual suicide, hide up a tree, blend in with rocks, hang upside down in caves or closets; she could become a pretend aristocrat, a benevolent but grandiose tyrant, a rude drunk, a humpbacked cripple, a dog howling in pain. But her favorite stance was inspired by the Popol-Vuh, the "bible" of her Maya ancestors on her mother's side—early humans squawking, chattering, hissing, complaining helplessly until they discovered the lofty art and religion of self-sacrifice, of a grand appeasement of the unknown forces in the universe. Here's a portrait of this stance:

Maya prominent personages of long ago appear on a platform in front of an audience; the man lacerates his penis and the woman her tongue with an obsidian lancer or a stingray spine. They then pull a rope made from the bark of a fig tree through their wounds letting the flowing blood fall into baskets full of paper strips. These strips are set afire to produce billows of black smoke which open the door into the otherworld, the world of the Vision Serpent; this supreme being then gives birth to a God through his wide open mouth. This God's job is to be petitioned, implored to maintain order on earth. Joanna as a young woman needed order imposed in her life, on her psyche. She fell in love with a very special man who seemed to have the power to grant her this wish.

This man, her late husband, was the father of one of her hosts who was on an afternoon hike; this man was the grandfather of two of the young people who were also hiking in the hills nearby. Perhaps they, along with the son's wife, would all end up listening to the same melodies from the treetop that Joanna had been listening to. Perhaps they would dance round and round the Maypole, the Axis Mundi, intertwined with silken red ribbons, not a rope made from the bark of a fig tree. They had no need to soak the ribbons in blood, to set them afire, to invite a demon to produce a savior. They only needed to laugh dance and sing connected to each other, to nature and to the world.

Still sitting quietly on the veranda, Joanna smiled, "Yes, that's how it should be!" She then imagined herself vigorously applauding all the powers that be, the powers of creation. It was then that she knew that it was this applause, this rough sort of music, that connected her to her stepson, his wife and their two children, her grandchildren.

LUCIFER'S ANGEL

My name is Bobby. I have a German last name but it's not pertinent to this story. I have shoulder-length blond hair. From behind, at a distance, as I walk dogs on the Upper East Side of New York City, I can be mistaken for an athletic woman. But I'm a man, a gay man. The story I have to tell is not about me. It is Harry's story as told to me by Old Harry himself, in bits and pieces over time. He could talk to me easily but we were never lovers. I loved him but I feel betrayed by him—why would he have an intimate relationship with a woman? An older woman, not even in his class. After all, we thought he was gay like the rest of us. Don't get me wrong. I like the woman but she could have had any man, why grab a gay man? What was the hold they had on each other—this is what I need to understand, what on earth was it? That's why I'm writing this.

First of all, I want you to know I'm not an ignorant man. I went to college. All of us did, but we didn't belong in the regular world. We didn't want what the mainstream wanted.

Let me begin with the story I'll call *The Fortress.* Harry and the woman I mentioned, Alma, went to

Puerto Rico. They visited El Moro, an ancient fortress in San Juan. Harry was so vivid with all the details I almost feel I was there myself, vendors all along the long drive to El Moro, selling fruit, sandwiches, hammocks, straw hats, caps with umbrellas riveted to the top. The most popular item was a bunch of plastic fruits. These were special gifts to be presented to all the invisible Gods all around them. They, the Gods, would then use them to appease bats or the ghosts of the dead. They should have bought tons of these!

Finally arriving at the rocky promontory overlooking the bay, they slipped in and out of dungeons, barracks, vaults. They stood unusually silent on all the lookouts. What *could* they possibly talk about? She was an elitist type talking with a slight English accent, had creamy white skin, genteel manners, a know-it-all serene expression on her face, never wearing jeans and tee-shirts. We all had read books but we belonged to the streets; she was in the clouds.

Then when she began to talk at the fortress, she wouldn't stop, "I guess you've never met a woman like myself. In fact, you probably haven't really loved any woman, have you?" Harry tried not to be led into an argument by not answering but she continued to taunt him. He felt she was challenging his identity.

Finally, he retorted, "I told you how its' been with me. Don't use it against me now."

"You mean how you're most comfortable with one-night-stands."

"No, it's hard for me to be close. Even when I'm

living with someone, I'm alone. I like it that way," Harry exclaimed a little impatiently. Yes, I can attest to that—even with all his friends around him Harry was a real loner. None of us knew what he really yearned for, what he dreamt about, what aches and pains he had. It's a wonder he confided in me about Alma—but what on earth was he looking for in her, why a "her"? Now look at me, I'm an open book—I'm hopelessly in love with a straight man but I still have my affairs as I think of him.

But back to my story—The bitch Alma continued in a sarcastic tone, "But you still get off pleasing others, ensnaring them with your servility, your amenability."

"What's with you anyway? Why are you nagging at me, what do you want from me? You said you just wanted a male companion, an escort for your outings, your travels. You said there were not strings attached."

Alma became softer, "I know, I know, it's just that I can't figure you out, sometimes you seem to really like me and other times you seem to be disdainful. I can ask you the same question, what do you want of me? I'd rather be anonymous than be in this never-never realm."

"That's what's wrong with you—you're always thinking, always studying people, examining me as if I were a bug!" And with that Harry began to walk faster and faster, ahead of her, with his long easy stride easily getting far away in no time. Before long she must have lost sight of his dark ponytail, his crisp white Guayabera shirt-jacket. It was then that she must have remembered he had, at her request, slung her heavy hobo bag onto his shoulder at the onset of their excursion. Her wallet, her passport, were all in it. It was possible that at that moment she thought he'd be waiting for her at the entrance at the bottom of the promontory, all sheepish and contrite. But he wasn't there. She must have sat on one of the benches thinking he'd gone to get the car at the nearby garage. Half an hour went by. No Harry. Maybe she walked to the garage, the car was gone. He was not at a nearby bar-restaurant. She returned to wait on the bench. Though somewhat alarmed, she was reassured, knowing she had a one-hundred dollar bill tucked away in an inner pocket, along with an extra credit card. Little did she know that Harry knew all about her safety devices, after all they shared the same hotel room, though not the same bed. She waited three hours before he showed up. Harry was surprised she was still there. He'd almost hoped she'd not only returned to the hotel but returned to New York. As she told him later, Alma was relieved to just have him in view; to see and enjoy his image was a great pleasure—the look of a gentleman pirate, a charming rogue, looking a little like Errol Flynn in some of his movies. This shows you how much older she was than our little group. Anyway, she must have felt a little like a coy victim, a captive. There was a strange power in being helpless, weak—it was disarming, perhaps even seductive at certain times.

As he drove up to where she sat she immediately noticed he looked wild-eyed, his complexion pale, almost greenish. As she sat down he handed her the bag gruffly saying, "Everything's there. Look for yourself. I can imagine what you've been thinking. You don't have to tell me—I know you as well as you know me, probably better, much better." She didn't look. She put the bag down on the floor. Putting one hand on her knee, he added, "Aren't you going to ask me where I've been?"

"Where?" she murmured almost indifferently.

"I visited a friend and then I visited one of my aunts who, by the way, looks like you, only smaller, older."

"What did they give you?"

"Tía gave me a glass of Portuguese rosé."

"And your friend?"

"I'm sure you know, don't you, or think you know."

What I don't understand as I tell this story is why didn't Harry pick up her bags and take her to the airport, why didn't Alma insist he do just that, what were they waiting for?

That night they had a suckling pig dinner. Harry was still strung out. All of us knew he was an on-and-off drug addict, usually only the soft stuff but he'd begun to sample heavier drugs. He kept putting a hand on her knee under the tablecloth, trying to stroke her inner thighs. Harry could be such a tease—in our circle we understood this and didn't take it seriously but Alma began to flip out, complaining he was acting hectic, agitated. He kept pressing one of his legs against hers. Once he took her hand and placed it on his crotch only to then push her hand away abruptly. Finally he put his arm around her neck pulling her head towards him. He kissed the top of her head and wept.

"I've told you we were eighteen offspring, and that I left home early, brought myself up, worked, went to college for awhile. All the time I thought my mother was a dirty whore because we were *so* many but my aunt told me today that we were all legitimate, some from mama's first marriage, some from papa's, and then those they had together. No one told me anything when I was growing up. I tormented her. I was cruel. I did terrible things to get back at her. I turned to boys for solace, flaunting my affairs in her face. Now she's dead, she can never forgive me."

Alma wiped his eyes, smoothed his hair, kissed the side of his face. I ask again, what the hell was she looking for, a pet, a doll, a lost son? I heard she had no children though married for many years before being widowed. Was he looking for a mother? I certainly don't like his referring to gayness as a kind of revenge, something pathological, bad, unnatural. We were meant to be who we are, we must accept this and respect nature. Something about that woman that is very disorganizing, making everything complicated, creating doubt, chaos. Why didn't she stick to her own kind?

Anyway, returning to the Caribe Hilton, they were immediately immersed in salsa music, the beat of percussion instruments, gourds, maracas, bongos, conga drums, claves and timbales. Wanting to hear the music more fully than possible from their room, Alma stepped out onto their terrace. Suddenly Harry slid the terrace door shut, locking it. She thought it was just a joke and smiled at him but he gave her a venomous look. She sat down, tried to relax but before long she got up and knocking on the glass she asked him to open the door.

He lay in bed smoking. He didn't move. She pounded on the glass. He didn't budge. She picked up a chair, hurling it at the glass but it was impenetrable.

Finally, he yelled, "What are you doing to me? I'm falling apart. Life was so simple before. I knew what I wanted to do and I just did it. Now I feel you gnawing at me, hungry, wanting something, wanting more."

Alma sat down saying nothing. Later, after he'd opened the door she told him that she knew she needed something but didn't know what it was. Sex? Not really. Love? Maybe. Companionship? Yes, but more really. She felt an attraction to him but it was more than sensuality. It was an attraction to something not of this world. Perhaps a spirit, a ghost, a shadow, a memory. Since her husband's death she felt a deep despair but it was lessened when she was with him. She quoted a guy called Søren Kierkegaard whom I'd never read myself, strange stuff:

> Despair is a Sickness in the Spirit, in the Self,...
>
> Despair at Not Being Conscious of Having a Self...
>
> Despair at *Not* Willing to Be Oneself;...
>
> Despair at *Willing* to Be Oneself.

"But that sounds like what *I* feel, that's so weird!" he exclaimed, embracing her.

I don't want to relate what happened next. It's embarrassing for our gay world. I know some of us have tried to become lovers of women, but we really should know better. Anyway, Harry became sexually aroused and with his usual fierce passion, he undressed her while she protested trying to tell him something. He tried to enter her but got in only a few inches. She was impenetrable. The walls of flesh had closed in upon each other. He stopped trying as she explained, "It's been like this for a long time. I've tried everything the doctors have recommended. Surgery is all that's left. That's why I've been so vacillating, wanting you, but being unable to receive you."

As his body relaxed Harry lay next to her, holding her close. Then laughing he blurted out, "We're birds of a feather, you and I."

• • •

You would think that incident showed them clearly that they didn't belong together but no, it brought them closer, almost as if they had been looking for an upside-down mirror image of themselves. Now *that's* a perversion, don't you think?

Okay, okay, I must continue my story. I think I'll call this next part *The Offspring*. Well, we already know she had no children, but did Harry? He called the boy his son but he wasn't. Apparently Harry saved him from the streets—a runaway or a throwaway of twelve roaming the streets of the Bronx selling himself to whoever wanted him. His name was Raymond. Harry registered him as his son in a public school with forged papers and began to guide him through his studies all the way through high school. The boy was destined to go to college, he was intelligent, eager to learn, ambitious. I don't know exactly what happened—who let who down and all that. My guess is that Harry fell in love with him, probably tried to seduce him, maybe even attacked him, and the kid flipped out. After that, out in the streets again, who knows what happened, how he ended up in prison, upstate. Well, whatever happened, Raymond eventually wanted Harry to visit him in jail. Harry took Alma with him for the visit, perhaps to look as if he'd changed, gone straight or something. I'm trying not to laugh and give Harry a break!

Before they could even enter the prison, they had to leave all their belongings in lockers, except for small change. Then after a quick body search and after filling out several forms, they were escorted by guards to a cafeteria area with tables, benches and food vending machines. As soon as an inner door was opened, Raymond sauntered over, dressed in the uniform of gray sweats. Alma muttered as he approached, "What a handsome boy!" He had coal-black hair, thick, wavy. She was surprised he hadn't gotten a drastic haircut. His skin was olive-toned, his smile wide, open, like that of a happy five year old child, upon seeing his parents. His large dark eyes seemed to see everything around him. After two minutes of greetings, Raymond began to treat Alma as if he'd known her all his life, was careful not to use crude words, was ready to help her up or down from her seat. It was hard for her to imagine he'd done anything so wrong it warranted his being imprisoned for five years. But she knew he'd been arrested as a drug dealer by an undercover cop.

"So, Alma," Raymond began jovially, "What do you see to like in my old man?"

She laughed nervously, not answering immediately. "Oh, I'm sorry," Raymond continued, "Perhaps I shouldn't ask, if it's too personal."

"No, no, it's okay. You *should* ask, you can ask anything you want. Harry is what I call a charming captivating enigma, a puzzle waiting to be put together, a riddle needing to be answered, a fable without a message."

"And you feel you're the one to solve it all, putting all the pieces in place?" Raymond persisted.

Alma nodded, smiling with embarrassment.

"I'd like to ask you another question, may I?"

"Yes, of course," she was impressed with his interest.

"Why do you think he's taken with *you*? I'm not asking *him* because I know what he'll say."

"Well," she began, surprised at how timid she felt, like a teenager, not like a very middle-aged woman. "I think he *wants* me to put the pieces together, to create a whole picture, that has within it a clear past, present and future for him to view, to enjoy, and for me to admire."

Raymond only smiled looking down at his can of soda. Harry kept looking furtively around him as if looking for an escape route. If he felt like a bug on the pin before, imagine what he felt like now with *both* of them scrutinizing him?

"Ray," Alma began softly, "You'll be paroled in a couple of years, what do you plan to do then?"

"Are you wondering if I intend to go back to living with pops, with Harry?"

"Well, yes."

"No, I'm too old, I want to try living alone and *not* coming back to this place," Raymond said with energy.

"What work can you do, how will you make your living?"

Ray grinned at her, "Well by now you must know what I do best, but I'm learning to be a car mechanic while I'm here.

I suppose that Alma had never seen Harry so completely humbled, so uncomfortable. Raymond kept glancing at him but hadn't addressed him directly. Suddenly out-of-the-blue, she blurted out, "Let's get it out into the open, what did Harry do to you?"

Raymond laughed, "What's with the psychologist bit?"

"Look, Harry and I are just good friends, but we know each other well. Nothing scares me."

Harry finally intervened, "Come on, Alma, what do you think I did? I tried to get into his pants!?"

Though she had suspected as much, Alma was taken aback, "How could you, he was like a son to you?"

"I loved him so much, more than I've ever loved anyone in the whole world."

"I know, I know, pops," and Raymond reached for one of Harry's hands. Harry did not move his hand away, but finally looked at Raymond fully in the face, "I'm sorry I chased you away, I didn't mean to hurt you."

"You're the one who should be in prison, not Ray," Alma muttered.

"I know, I know," Harry began slowly removing his

hand from under Raymond's and turning himself totally around to face Alma, "But you, what are you doing with me, what blackness within you is giving you your kicks by being with me?"

Alma said nothing. This time Raymond reached for *her* hand. After patting both of her hands, he said, "Welcome to the club, Alma, you're one of us."

• • •

I wish I'd met Raymond. Harry always kept him under wraps. Anyway, he caught something about Alma I hadn't seen—that she wasn't just strange, she had a deep, dark side. The three of them were in essence a kind of Holy Trinity, Father, Son and the Ghost. You see, as weird as they were, you know—breaking the law, being willing to either hurt others or willingly turn a blind eye—there was something of the God-Whisperer about each of them. Mind you, I'm not religious but I was brought up in a family full of devotion to God. All this makes me wonder, maybe I'm immoral. No, not because I'm gay. You know that man I love so hopelessly, well, he has a young son of ten or so. I've befriended him. He calls me Uncle Bobby and loves me, hugging me all the time, following me around. Would I ever want to prey on him? I wonder. I really, really wonder. I worry that because we live on the outskirts of society, almost like outcasts, not abiding by the usual rules, we may get to believe that anything goes. Could it be that Alma doesn't belong to the mainstream either? She looks mainstream, genteel, ladylike, a retired teacher. I must say I really don't know much about her—two marriages, the first in her teens, an adventurer father and an artist mother. Oh, well, let's just continue.

I'd like to call my next Harry story *Beach Boys*. Once again he and Alma are traveling, this time in Acapulco. They stayed at *The Princess Resort* which included swimming pools, many restaurants, and access to miles of beaches with horses, dune buggies and boats for hire.

On the third day of sitting on the sand under an umbrella, a herd of lean brown boys, from twelve to fourteen years of age, descended upon all the visitors. They were selling refreshments, painted gourds, woven baskets and straw hats, necklaces made of dried nuts, knitted vests and bikinis for the very slender, certainly not for Alma or Harry. It was probably the boys' families who created all the wares they were peddling. Harry began to joke around with one of the older boys. Alma began to get suspicious because she questioned Harry repeatedly, asking if they were exchanging secret messages. He only laughed. Then she asked if the boy, Manuel, had handed Harry something. He denied receiving anything. Then she insisted they not go to the beach anymore—she preferred they sit around one of the pools. Together, they chose one that featured a bar set up under an overhang of rocks. The swimmers didn't even have to get out of the water to order a drink. Harry was a little embarrassed at Alma's outfit. She floated around the turquoise waters looking like a giant black fly in her black chiffon pants and shirt worn over a black bathing suit.

Then Harry began to disappear for hours on end. Alma must have known he was at the beach. One day he didn't return to their room till evening just as the peacocks in the gardens unfurled their feathers, as they rotated gracefully in one spot, as they began their screechy bedtime song.

"Where are all your belongings, your shorts, shirts, sandals? Where's your gold chain, bracelet?" she asked contemptuously. He was only wearing a jockstrap. He had sand in his hair and bruises all over his torso.

Sighing sheepishly, mischievously, he muttered, "Believe it or not, I was mugged, knocked out cold."

"And, of course, raped," she continued icily.

"Maybe a little, but at least I wasn't murdered and made to disappear. Aren't you happy to see me alive and relatively well?"

Alma screamed at him, "How did you figure out how to open my room safe—some of my money is missing. Why did you need more cash—you had plenty of your own when we arrived?"

"Well, if you must know, I wanted to help those boys down at the beach."

"By just giving them money?" she queried.

"Yes, why not?"

Once again Alma was sarcastic, "Then they jumped you, wanting more, is that your tale of woe?"

"Not exactly."

"Well, you might as well tell me," she said quietly, probably realizing once again that she had no claim on him. After all they weren't even *real* lovers. Harry told me they had fun though, romping around naked like kids.

"The truth is that I offered Manuel more money if he sold me something special to smoke. He agreed and I followed him to a hut several miles down the beach. It just didn't work out the way I thought it would."

"Aren't you angry Manuel tricked you, betrayed you?"

"No, it was fun while it lasted. Anyway, I did get my smokes. It was worth every cent. It wasn't Manuel who did me in, it was those others who waited for me as I headed back here."

Can you picture Old Harry, his large muscular body in effect only in a loincloth? Alma must have found him totally enchanting, tanned, dusty, his eyes glowing, happy to be back with a caring person. I wonder, though, if she was concerned that Harry may have been having sex with a fourteen year old. It certainly bothers me. I don't like the idea of gay men getting a reputation as pedophiles. Would it bother me otherwise? Yes, I think so—even if a boy has gone astray and the sex is freely offered, he's only a child, a baby who doesn't really understand how by bruising his body, he's bruising his thoughts, his memories. Don't ask me why this upsets me. I don't want to go there—I've never believed that catharsis is good for the soul.

The bottom line is I don't want to judge Harry, to maybe get to dislike him. I never questioned his basic integrity until that Alma popped into our world, turning it upside down with her restless search for God knows what, asking for nothing but wanting it all, wanting everything.

I almost wish there was nothing more to that day in Acapulco, that it had ended with the reunion in the hotel room. But no, Harry had more to tell. Anyway, he gallantly invited her to dine out with him in an elegant restaurant along the beach, of course, on an IOU. They walked and walked, both dressed in silken whites, slacks and billowy low-cut tunics. They carried their Greek-styled sandals by the long laces.

"We're almost there. I was told it's right after the ruins of an old church," Harry put one arm around her waist.

Alma muttered, "I could walk like this forever, listening to the sea, looking at the sea. Sometimes it looks as if it had frantic fingers that are searching for the shore, fingers that need to caress the shore.

Harry laughed, squeezed her closer to his body till they were moving as one.

Harry told me, with awe, that that night was one of the most beautiful of his life, all because he pretended to be a man in love with a woman, a woman he would love forever, being true to her always. What crap, have you ever heard anything more fucking ridiculous! What a hypocritical ending to a perfect day of greed, of lust, pure abandon! Why did Harry have to tell me his story, what did he expect from me, what was he looking for in my eyes?

There's another question I'm hesitant to ask. It's difficult even to phrase. It has to do with all of us who are not mainstream, who are not joiners, you know, people who are basically outsiders, maybe even misfits. Considering that it is harmful, dangerous, to live without structure, conventions, does this make us *too* free, *too* prone to improvise, to experiment, to fall prey to evil, to Satan's beckonings? In loving Alma on that night in Acapulco was Harry's wishing, ever so simply, for a solid framework within which to live?

• • •

I'm calling this last segment *The Messenger.* This time Harry's story is set in the Bronx, New York. Frankly, I'm surprised Alma would even set foot in that borough, so full of the forgotten, the poor, but that's where Harry worked, and lived, when he wasn't in Manhattan, with Alma, in her apartment. By then, she had latched onto him so tightly that if she wanted to be with him, she'd have to be willing to go anywhere, at any time. In a way she acted a little like a protector, a guard of some sort, guardian, I guess.

Harry and Alma went by taxi to an immense housing project near the Bronx Zoo. It looked like a factory for the manufacture of strollers, bicycles, and shopping carts. The atmosphere was that of chaotic joviality. The walls of the unsteady elevators were decorated with names of affection, pet names like Bobo, Rusty, Baby Face, Big Mama, Tubby, Conejo. The apartment they went to was quite nice: new, bare windows letting in the sunlight, linoleum tiles on the floors that looked like real wood. A lovely young woman in a fluffy yellow sweater opened the door: slender, bright-eyed, dark hair and eyes. She offered them a goblet of dark rum. Before long, her boyfriend emerged from the bedroom dressed all in black, with one eye that didn't stay put in its socket. There was a lump growing on the side of his slender neck. He was all smiles when he saw Harry, embracing him heartily. But they hardly knew each other. Alma learned later that the young man was feeling Harry s body for weapons or wires, after all Harry was there to purchase drugs. Apparently, judging by all her questions to Harry, she hoped it was only grass he wanted but her suspicions had already been aroused by his behavior at times, making her afraid he'd be buying cocaine or crack. Harry told me how one night she'd awakened alone in his apartment and had gone looking for him at all his friends' apartments in the building. Finding him a glassy-eyed zombie, she'd forced him to go back with her, all the while berating him.

But let's get on with *The Messenger.* The four of them continued drinking rum as they conversed. While Harry and Enrique talked quietly, Susanna told Alma she had two young children living with her mother. She hoped to one day get them back when she cleaned up her act. Alma asked her what she meant, "What is it you need to clean up?"

Susanna laughed, "I like guys a lot. They like me. I'm worth a lot to them, much more than I was to my deadbeat husband. But, of course, it wasn't good for the kids. They're better off with mama, now that papa is gone, thank God."

"I see," Alma murmured, gathering Susanna was a prostitute.

"Yep, I just need a little more time, I need more money and then I'm going to school for some computer skills. By the way, are you Harry's 'old lady'?"

"What do you mean?"

"You know, taking care of him," Susanna said.

"We each have our own apartment and Harry has a well-paying job."

"I hope you're not shocked at my asking but though you're very attractive, you're much older and you're out of his league," again Susanna was totally matter-of-fact. "I'll bet you don't even smoke cigarettes, right?"

"No, I never learned to inhale but I tried to learn many times," Alma chuckled, "But as you see, I love to drink."

"I won't ask you what else you love—you can't possibly be without vices!" Susanna laughed but the sound she made was more like a cackle.

Enrique, Susanna and Harry exchanged glances—the bottle of rum and glasses were put away. Alma went to the bathroom, probably thinking she and Harry would be leaving soon. When she returned, Enrique and Susanna were on the couch puffing on a pipe they were sharing. Susanna's skirt was raised, she was wearing no underwear. Harry was standing in a corner, leaning against the wall as he stuck a needle into one of his forearms. He said that even as he slowly slumped to the floor, he'd always remember the look of horror on Alma's face. How could he forget her screeching out his name as she rushed to his side on the floor. He continued to hear her voice but it seemed to be coming from far away, "Wake up, don't die, it's not worth it!" He knew from experience that Enrique and Susanna would be lost in a vacuum of sensation, like the dead in one of the circles of hell doomed to forever experience only pleasure and nothing else. He had come to prefer to feel the peace of nothingness, the consciousness, the wakefulness of nothingness. But he hated worrying Alma, he hadn't expected his extreme reaction to the shot. He fought to become alert again. Slowly he allowed himself to be helped to his feet, led out of the apartment, into the elevator and soon after led into a gypsy cab.

After a long nap in his apartment, he awakened more himself but still unusually tranquil.

"I hadn't planned on doing that but Ricky gave it to me as a gift, to try it."

"You scared me half to death," Alma began, "how could you have done this to yourself, to me; what did you inject, heroin?"

"I'm sorry. I wasn't thinking. I was just curious."

"Just curious!" Alma was almost shouting, "My God, it's like being curious about death, about trying it out, just a little bit. Aren't you happy with what you and I have, a friendship with no strings attached, no responsibilities, just being there for each other."

"It has nothing to do with you, with our friendship."

"Oh come on, we're together so much of the time. Are you needing more space, more alone time, perhaps?"

Harry was perplexed, "What makes you ask that?"

"Well, you've been in a relationship with me for quite some time—kind of a training, a preparation for..."

"No, I'm fine, don't nag at me about something else. I don't want the whole body, the whole soul bit, that's just too scary. I like one at a time, please. Let me hold on to something that's just mine!"

Alma didn't respond right away. Maybe she was hurt. I would think she'd be *very* hurt. Then, after a few moments, she asked, "So, you're protecting yourself from being taken over, by taking heroin?"

Harry caressed her face, patting her hair back into place, "That was just a one-time deal, nothing more. I'm sorry, sorry, so sorry you had to see it."

You know, as an observer and listener, once again I was astounded. What is the matter with that woman, where has she been, where did she come from? Why hasn't she gotten it—he's an addict, a conniver, a liar. Of course, he is charming, lovable, but really no good, like the rest of us living on the fringes. We tell ourselves society has rejected us but let's face it, we like it that way. It's so freeing to be shunned—we owe nobody, we can lick our wounds to our heart's content. Maybe that's why I dislike Alma, she's not rejecting of us. She almost makes me feel guilty, regretful.

Well, in a million years I'll bet you'll never guess how this story ends. It was a shock to me, to Harry, to our whole gang. There's nothing more to say except to just tell you the end. Brace yourself. I was actually nearby. I was almost present.

A few weeks after the Enrique incident, Harry and Alma took a walk in Central Park, from one end to the other, north to south. They stopped at the Boathouse Restaurant for scallops and martinis. Their walk to my apartment, way over on East 60th Street, was more of a dance to the music of their own laughter. From time to time their hips knocked rhythmically against each other, almost knocking each other over. My apartment is five flights up a narrow marble staircase, not difficult to climb, unless the climber is impaired in some way. Perhaps the drinks had relaxed Alma too much, who knows. Harry said she was holding on to the banister on one side and his arm on the other. They reached the last step, she let go of the banister. She also let go of his arm. Down she went, backwards, down the whole last flight of stairs. Her head thumped upon the indented ancient edges of each step. She lay limp at the bottom. Harry screamed, " Bobby, Bobby, call an ambulance. Oh, my God, my God, why did she let go of me. Why did I allow her to let go?" He picked her up in his arms and carried her into my apartment. She was lifeless. She was no more. She was dead.

Was this her escape, her revenge, her sacrifice, was she a messenger from the beyond? If so, what was her message, I feel there is one, but what? What? Was it that we should see the hopelessness of *not* making connections, deep connections? Was it that we should learn to fight against the emptiness of living in limbo? Was it that we should *not* accept being outsiders, outcasts? But somehow this all seems so meager, certainly it's not enough to suffer for. Certainly it can't be enough to die for, or can it?

PALACE ON THE RIVER

Scent of the Jungle
One Step Up
The Golden Key
Beauty Parade
Mannequins in the Window
Sucking at the Jugular
Pandora's Curse
Phantasms

Scent of the Jungle

Everyday in the past few weeks she came and sat on a bench in front of the edifice where patients usually wait for their ambulette, access-a-ride, or car service. She was small, sturdy. Her spiked hair fanned outwards and upwards exposing a sloping forehead and large ears. Her resemblance to a rodent of sorts was completed by her upturned nose, pebbly black eyes and an overbite. Hieroglyphic designs adorned the borders of her long dark skirt and tunic and naked toes had been painted on her white sneakers. She always carried a red notebook and a long black pencil. Sometimes she scribbled furiously as she turned page after page, her shield-like giant bracelet gleaming in the gloomy alleyway full of the grunts and squeaks of vehicles. What did she see to draw, to write about in that crowd of human beings on wheels and sticks?

Sometimes she walked around within the edifice with its white walls, white dresses and jackets. No one stopped her or questioned her. Perhaps they didn't see her.

"What's your name?" she asked a young blond man

wheeling himself around in his chair. In the last few weeks she'd seen him many times. He was always on the move. He stopped, startled. He had been about to wheel right by her, almost right through her, "Roland, what's yours?"

"Vivian," then after a pause she continued, "How come you're allowed to roam the halls? I've seen you on almost every floor. Are you as invisible as I am?"

He laughed, pleased with the idea. "They're still trying to figure out why I can't walk. I've been here weeks and weeks—this test and that test on and on."

"What do you think it could be?"

"Who knows!" Roland laughed again, "But one of the residents thinks it's a form of suicide."

Vivian's eyes opened wide, "Did you try killing yourself, perhaps by trying to jump from a window?"

"Oh no, no, nothing like that, though I imagine myself flying out of the window on great wings and swooping down on the river below. I love watching the seagulls doing just that from my window."

"Maybe they can carry you away from here, ferry you across to a better place."

"What a neat idea! By the way I love your painted feet but I would have painted wings on <u>my</u> shoes. But to each his own, right?"

Vivian smiled. "Forgive me for asking but why would that young doctor even use the word 'suicide'?"

"Oh, he never used the word 'suicide.' He just gave me some hocus pocus about my body destroying itself from within, something about some cells going crazy, running amok, something like friendly fire!"

"Your _immune_ cells, at least some of them right?" Vivian muttered. "They must think you have an autoimmune disease."

"Who knows?" Roland seemed indifferent. "There's nothing _I_ can do about it.

"So you fly around the halls," Vivian sighed.

"Yep, be seeing you!" and Roland wheeled himself swiftly away.

Sometimes Vivian visited some of the rooms, idly at first, then as if she were looking for something, or someone. The single rooms were not only for private patients but also for those with infections related to orthopedic surgeries or to severe joint diseases. But it was not a single room she was looking for—slowly she began to realize that the room she was looking for, the room she must enter, was a double room. In the meantime, she went into a storage room that had been converted into an emergency patient room. It contained a bed, a sink and a commode. The walls were plastered with vivid watercolor paintings; they were portraits of the same woman, probably self-portraits by the patient. Vivian guessed they were rendered by looking into a magnifying glass for the features were grossly exaggerated, distorted. But it was some kind of strange energy that turned the natural exaggerations into pure grotesqueness. The patient lay in bed with an intravenous line attached to one arm. The line was attached to a rack where three plastic bags hung, all different fluid antibiotics. Vivian wondered if the self-portraits were a result of her illness, her raging infection which could lead to amputations or even death, or had she always been an artist of the bizarre.

"Hello, I'm Vivian. Is there anything I can do for you?" Vivian enjoyed pretending to be a volunteer patient-helper—it was ironic for she knew she was far from being a kind helping hand.

The woman only vaguely acknowledged her as she muttered more to herself than to her, "How do you like my umbilical cord? It reaches up to the tree of life as I dance and dance, winding and unwinding myself, tangled, yet always untangled, yet too tangled to tango!"

Vivian only nodded, smiling to herself as she walked quietly out of the room. Yes, it takes two to tango, she thought, as she now began her search for the two sisters, Una and Tess.

• • •

"If you hadn't been so busy telling me what I'm feeling you wouldn't have lost your balance!" Tess almost shouted at her older sister Una. They had had a fall in Guatemala, at the Maya archaeological site of Tikal. They had been climbing the pyramid called *The Grand Jaguar* and had ended up in a heap together. As a consequence Una's dormant rheumatic disease had flared up and Tess had broken her ankle in three places.

Una shot back, "And if you hadn't been so eager to once again tell me how awful, how overbearing I was, you wouldn't have twisted your ankle and fallen on top of me!" After a pause she continued, "But then that's what you've done all your life, follow me around taking a free ride on my back."

"That's not fair!" Tess retorted, "You yourself seduce me to be at your side and then you chase me away."

Both fell silent for a few minutes totally exasperated with being in bed, in a hospital, both unable to even walk to the adjoining bathroom. They were both very attractive in their early twenties. It was difficult to tell who was the oldest—they almost looked like twins, long hair, soft features, trim figures. The main difference was that Una had a remoteness about her glance while Tess had the piquancy of one who was fully in the moment. In any case Una would have to miss the beginning of the fall semester as a high school literature teacher and Tess would have to temporarily suspend her practice as a physical therapist.

Sighing, as she pulled her long brown hair roughly back into a knot, Una asked, "I don't remember what feelings I was attributing to you."

Tess turned her head to face Una, her black eyes cold, aggrieved, "You said that since papa left me out, preferring you, I'm always competing with you for a man's attention. I guess you were thinking of that guy we met in the hotel. For your information he was interested only in me from the very beginning.

"You don't even know what you do," Una scoffed, "You're so full of old gripes, the poor little abandoned waif!"

"Ha!" Tess snorted, "And you didn't feel left out by mama? I was her favorite, her baby. Just remember, you talked me into coming with you to that infernal Maya site and why? Because you wanted to connect with mama even if only with her ancestors—how pathetic is that?" If you could, you'd bring her back to life!

Una pressed the button that propped her up in the bed as if preparing for battle but then she didn't say anything. Out of the blue she remembered one day, not long ago, when she'd said to Tess, "Tell me something nice" and Tess answering "I can't think of a thing!" It was then that their door slowly opened and an apparition appeared. It was Vivian.

• • •

Vivian walked in without making a sound. Her beady eyes glaring, her nostrils flared open. Without waiting for anyone to say anything she pulled up a chair and sat down at the foot of both beds, between the two of them. "Think of me as an emissary from your dead mother. I have a message for you. It is in the form of a story, a fable. You are required to listen." As she spoke she brandished her giant mirrored bracelet around, directing its glint into their eyes, mesmerizing them. Her winged hair grew in its thickness, totally framing her presence. The sisters could do nothing but listen to the unexpectedly melodious voice. No one had ever held their attention to such an extent, not their father, mother, any teacher, any piece of music or painting, certainly not each other.

• • •

Once upon a time there lived a young princess in the jungle who did not know she was a princess. In fact no one knew, not even her mother. She rode on crocodiles to cross the deep rivers and she slept next to large striped and spotted cats. But snakes frightened her. She froze when she saw one, their yellow eyes burning her with their cold flames. Her mother was always hard at work bringing civilization to the small towns in the area—building houses, chapels, schools, roads, corrals for animals, and creating fish ponds, gardens, clothing and grocery shops. No matter how hard she tried she couldn't get her daughter to help. The mother feared for the girl's future but after awhile she forgot about her, as she herself grew as a leader, a chief, a shaman and gained many followers. They worked hard to maintain their independence from the central government as well as from all the distant governments around them.

But one day a governor from the capital descended into the village square with a small army, rounding up everyone, threatening them with annihilation if they didn't kneel before him and kiss his feet. The mother-chieftain refused, waving her machete and declaring that even if they took all their blood, leaving them limp and pale, they would never bow down to their authority. The governor didn't want to shed blood. The whole country was drenched in blood from the time of the ancient Indian Kingdoms to modern time with all the battles for liberty, for land, for power. It seemed to be their legacy.

There was always some grievance to kill for, to die for, to shed still more blood. Was it the curse of their ancient Gods who in trying to create a superior being who could sing their praises they stumbled upon the precious component—blood. Its beautiful flow and hue became the ultimate proof of loyalty to the Gods, through self-sacrifice, self-mutilation and finally through the sacrifice of others. In addition, the extreme loss of blood created an addiction to the endorphins released, giving them an irresistible pleasure.

Suddenly the governor saw the girl, the young princess with her long tangled hair, wide innocent eyes dressed only in pounded bark, and leaves strung together with vines. A baby jaguar leaned against her legs purring lightly.

"I will spare your village on one condition: I will enrich you, build palaces for you, anything you want—all I want is that girl and the right to supervise your work, our work, for one year. Bring her to my camp by nightfall."

Though the mother feared for her daughter, she saw no other way out of their problem. She also didn't want more bloodletting, though she was willing to do battle to the end. The governor seemed a gallant man. He might even do her daughter some good, grounding her, making her more practical more realistic and accessible. Perhaps she would learn to dress properly, to eat with utensils and to use a toilet. Of course she knew she would be deflowered and trained in the ways of a courtesan. But then she herself had been married off at twelve, already pregnant. Her daughter had just turned thirteen. It was no big deal. Just a little more blood for one night and, of course, later on when the babies came. The mother stepped forward and loudly accepted the governor's proposal.

• • •

Una tried to say something but no words came out the way it sometimes happens in a dream when someone tries to scream. Tess had tears in her eyes but they couldn't drop down on her cheeks, her eye sockets becoming glistening still pools of water. Vivian looked closely at them, almost with sympathy and then she continued.

• • •

The princess did not fight her mother. She understood perfectly well what was happening and what she had to do. She set her pet jaguar free and put on the long white dress with lace ruffles at the neck and at the hem, each ruffle embroidered with flowers by her mother. The dress had been stored in a wicker chest for her daughter's wedding. Then the mother herself gently adorned her daughter with dangling filigree earrings, bracelets and matching silver sandals. The governor fell even more in love with her than he had at first sight. He was as gentle with her on their first night as his ardent nature permitted but the girl hated the nights, the bed, the man.

She longed for her big cats with their clean earthy aroma. It was so superior to the turgid aroma of masculine sweat mixed with aromatic oils. But she didn't run away, and the governor didn't leave after the year was up. Eventually, she gave birth to a boy, then another. Both boys died of no apparent reason and their bodies disappeared without a trace. It was rumored that she fed them to her cats in the jungle, not wanting to put them into a dark hole in the ground.

One day the governor's rival and brother arrived on the scene wanting to take over the whole territory, to add it to his own neighboring domain. They battled each other in wrestling matches but no winner could be proclaimed. The rival brother was banished back to where he came from. But he continued to challenge his brother every few years, each time with more deadly force so that eventually they were spilling each other's blood, slowly depleting themselves and each other.

One day a third brother appeared, one they thought would never amount to anything, a short man with no hair, many gold teeth, with freckles and blind-looking grey eyes. In addition, he always had a viper wrapped around his neck and chest. Without saying a word he shot the governor in the legs and dumped him on a nearby island which housed whole families of crocodiles. Then still without a word, he whisked the princess away to a far off land. Oddly enough she loved him immediately despite the clinging viper. Together, the man and the snake, smelled of the earth, the dust, the dew. They reminded her of her jungle. She was so satisfied she went on to give birth to two daughters who are now grownup.

• • •

Una tried to move her frozen face, to smile but only one side of her face managed to curl upward. Tess coughed a little or gurgled. It was hard to tell what sounds she was trying to make. Vivian patted both sisters' feet as she continued.

• • •

You two women are old enough to know better. As has been said so many times by many, it is time to give up childish things, childish ways. It is time to pick yourself up, dust yourself off and live your lives. If you don't, you're going to get sicker and sicker, and in the end, you will kill yourselves off.

Then giving them both many rough strokes on their feet and legs, Vivian rose to her feet and left the room

• • •

Una and Tess stared at each other. Una found her voice. She whispered, "Who was she, what was she—a bat from hell or from an insane asylum?"

Tess whispered back, tears wetting her cheeks, "But why did we listen for so long?" Why did she hold our attention, our very souls?"

"I don't know," Una murmured, realizing how rare

it was for her to admit she didn't know everything. "It almost feels as if mama was here embracing us both, but yet this doesn't make any sense at all."

Tess could only quietly weep.

After a few moments, Una stretched one arm towards Tess, "I wish I could touch you, to reach your hand, to grip it tightly, to never let it go."

Tess then sobbed out loud, "Yes, I'd like that."

It was all that was necessary for the moment. It was the nicest thing Tess could have answered to Una's everlasting request, "Tell me something nice."

One Step Up

Vivian sat idly on her bench in front of the special edifice she'd chosen as her second home. Nothing much had changed in her appearance except she seemed a little tired. There were a few gray hairs at her temples highlighting the spiked fanned-out hair, waxed at the pointed ends. Cleanliness was important to her—the white hieroglyphic designs on her outfit were never smudged. Somehow her overbite was becoming more prominent—perhaps because her face was thinner.

The automatic sliding door of the edifice opened and a woman emerged onto the sidewalk. She walked slowly, propelling herself forward on two crutches by pivoting her wide hips and her locked kneed legs. The driver of one of the parked cars in the alleyway stepped out and ran to help her. The woman waved him away by impatiently nodding her head and frowning. He obeyed and returned to the car, opening the front door. Eventually she lowered herself, buttocks first, onto the passenger seat, handing him the crutches. Then with her own hands she lifted her legs into the vehicle.

As he closed the door, the driver asked, "What did

the doctor say, madame?"

"I must return in two weeks, have my knees defused and then get two new knees, replacements," she answered coldly, a little out of breath.

• • •

Two weeks later, Vivian visited Kivi Niemi, before the surgery. She entered the corner private room on one of the top floors. It had views of the river both north and east. She glided in, sat down on an easy chair and waited for the woman to awaken.

Kivi opened her eyes. Seeing Vivian she growled, "What are you doing in my room? This is not a costume party!"

"You're wrong—that's exactly what it is. You're disguised as a crippled superwoman and I'm disguised as an underworld messenger trying to prove something about why people become ill."

Immediately combative Kivi answered, "For your information I got juvenile rheumatoid arthritis when I was ten. I had nothing to do with becoming sick. Even now I want nothing better than to be able to walk without crutches, no matter how slowly, to walk with legs that bend. Now, get out of my room!"

Vivian didn't budge, "Were you always a nasty person, or is it due to your pain, your humiliation, your disability?"

Kivi seemed pleased by the question, "Not nasty, realistic. Anyway, what do you know? Let me tell you a little story. Then maybe you'll understand and leave me be!"

"Not long ago a couple took me out to Chinatown for dinner. It was an arranged public relations event since I came from far away, since I was in the state I am. The man went off to park the car and I was left with his poor young wife who didn't know what to make of me, not even what to say, though I was only a few years older than she was. She was embarrassed by me as if I were ancient.

Awkwardly she began to lead me inside the restaurant, but there it was, one short step, up to the door. I was exasperated. I had made it clear to them I couldn't navigate *any* steps! But she was so frightened I felt sorry for her. So, I tried putting one leg up on a slant while leaning into the building but there just wasn't enough support to allow for my weight while I lifted the other leg. The little woman didn't have the strength to lift my body upwards as I maneuvered my legs. She suggested we wait for her husband. I couldn't stand feeling, looking so helpless. Not wanting to wait, I kept on struggling, kept on failing. Hot, sweaty, breathless, I felt like a cartoon baby bear trying to wiggle out of a pail where I was stuck, ass down. There's nothing like a cartoon for depicting disturbances in the balance between man and the world. It's in cartoons one sees the plight of Sisyphus, persistence in the face of hopelessness. The wife didn't want to look at my struggle—*she* felt helpless, ashamed, hating the empathy that led to identifying with freaks.

Finally the woman, frantic by now, announced

she'd get help from within the restaurant. A waiter came outside. When he saw me he threw up his arms screeching something in his language. My little hostess beseeched him to help, offering him a twenty-dollar bill. Imagine! That's how desperate she was! Stuffing the bill into his jacket, he gruffly tried to pull me up, yanking, pulling. Finally he rudely declared, "Too heavy!" and began to go back into the restaurant. By then I'd had it with all the ineptness. I detained him by holding onto his arm, "Let me show you how to help." Patiently I indicated he get behind me, crouching, that he embrace me right above the waist and then that he slowly straighten himself up, lifting me upwards at the same time. The first attempt almost succeeded. Encouraged he crouched even more, and smiling, sure he would succeed, he lifted me up the one step. The two of them laughed heartily together. By the time the husband returned, the waiter was plying us with hot tea and little dumplings. All was well.

So, what do you think now—am I nasty or just merely realistic? I don't really care about your answer—please leave!"

"Not quite yet," Vivian murmured. Then floating over to Kivi's side, she added, "You're quiet satisfied with yourself, aren't you? In a way you have the world at your feet. You're like a giant jigsaw puzzle that needs to be put together. You keep people working on you, mystified by you, breaking their heads over you, their pleasure of success held hostage by you. But haven't you paid too high a price to achieve this power?"

"What are you saying? That I've become a wreck so

as to lord it over people?"

"Not necessarily."

"What then? That I use being a wreck to captivate people's attention?"

"Not really," Vivian muttered softly.

Kivi pulled herself up by the swaying bar overhead. Then resting on her elbows as she raised the top of her bed upwards, electronically, she glared at Vivian, "Since you seem to know it all, *you* tell me what you mean."

"Mean by what?" Vivian laughed.

"Now who's playing games?" What you said about my paying a price as if I had something to do with creating my crippled state!"

"Isn't it a terrible, terrible life you have?" Vivian almost whispered.

"It's the only one I have—what would you have me do?" Kivi's face was twisting this way and that.

Vivian waited, returning to the chair at the foot of the bed.

"Well, what should I be doing differently?" Kivi persisted, her voice tremulous.

"When did you lose your faith, your trust in people? When did you separate yourself from caring hands, at what age, at what too early an age?"

"I don't know what you're talking about!" But Kivi's voice was choked. "As far back as I remember, I've relied on myself, even as a small child."

"Who consoled you when you bruised your knees in a fall? Who wiped the tears off your face and extolled you to be more careful next time?"

"No one had to. Why should they? I wasn't an idiot, a retardate you know!"

"That's right, but you weren't Superwoman either."

"I don't understand, "Kivi's voice was almost a complaint, a whining. She closed her eyes, clenching her hands, stiffening her arms, causing the arteries in her neck to stand out as her jaws clamped tightly together. You could almost hear the grinding of her teeth.

"Poor little Kivi!" Vivian murmured as she rose to her feet and headed for the door. As she stepped out into the hall she heard the beginning of sobs, as yet gurgled, strangled. Vivian knew that soon, in time, they would become wails, loud wails. Vivian also knew that it would be the first time Kivi Niemi had ever cried for herself, for all that had been lost and for all others who suffered.

The Golden Key

Vivian didn't know why she had chosen to do what she did, to haunt the halls of the palace on the river. All she knew was that she had to. It wouldn't be for long, her time on earth was limited, coming to an end—of that she was certain. Where, when had it all begun? Oddly enough not that long ago. She knew nothing of what had happened all the years before it all began, she couldn't remember, no matter how hard she tried. This is what she remembers.

She came to, awakened, whatever, huddled in an over-soft loveseat. Her thoughts were strange. She was thinking how she'd always found a certain drama very exciting, one where someone was doomed but totally puzzled by what had led him or her to their predicament. Now here she was in the same predicament, sinking deeper and deeper into the little sofa as time passed.

She had no strength, no stamina left, losing weight with every long sigh. She had no appetite, only nausea but when she threw up there was only yellow saliva. The windows in the living room where she sat were boarded up. A dim light burned in a dilapidated lamp. She remembered shutting off the water in all the taps because the drips nagged at her, criticizing her, resenting her every thought, her every breath, almost acting like a countdown to the end.

Once in awhile she'd stagger up, stumble into the bathroom to look at herself in the mirror, to see if she was still there. She'd had to wedge a broken-off broom from the top of the medicine cabinet to the ceiling where a leak upstairs had loosened the plaster which threatened to fall upon her head whenever she sat on the toilet.

She didn't know why she thought so but she was sure that before long the door would burst open and she'd be dragged away. What had she done? What evil had she perpetrated? She had an overwhelming sense of guilt—it was eating at her, devouring her. She had no inkling of being entitled to love, to thrive, to enjoy anything. Now and then she vaguely remembered living a long time in another place. Somehow she knew this place had been taken away from her, along with everything that was hers. Did she have anything left? Money? Clothes? How long had she been in this small ugly place?

There was a knock on the door. How did they get in? The front door of the building was locked or were they living within the building itself? She wondered how she knew the front door downstairs was locked.

Then the knock came again, this time louder. She crept down the hall and looked through the peephole. No one was there. She returned to the loveseat and hugged a cushion. The knock came again. Then a kick to the door and more knocking, over and over again. The knob turned this way and that way, more knocking, more kicking. This time she ran down the hall shouting, "Who's there? Who are you?" There was silence. She stood at the door for a long time. Finally when she looked through the peephole there was only darkness in the hallway.

She wanted to talk to herself but she didn't know how to address herself. Oddly enough she felt clearer in the head, not so weak, faint and nauseated. She went into the kitchen to see if she could find evidence of who she was. Lapsang Suchon teabags. She made a cup of tea. Suddenly she wanted it with scotch. Sure enough, in the cupboard she found a bottle of Teachers. Stoned wheat crackers and Brie were next. Rice pudding with nutmeg on top, a compote of fresh fruits soaked in an orangey liquor followed. Who had put these items in the kitchen? Who knew her palate so well?

Where was her handbag? She left the kitchen returning to the living room. No bag. The books she found were *The Dilemma of Identity, The Search for the Self, Human Destructiveness.* She knew nothing of what they could have been saying. She looked for the closet. It was next to the bathroom. Looking inside she saw an old shapeless leather jacket with a Ferragamo label. In the deep pockets she found hundreds of dollars, but no wallet, no identification. On the few hangers there were duplicates of what she was wearing, black skirts, black tunics, all with white hieroglyphic borders. On the floor of the closet sat three pairs of white sneakers, all with toes painted on them. Around the necks of one of the tunics hung a long beaded necklace with a pouch-like leather pendant. Hooked onto the pouch was an immense silver bracelet, a cuff really, in the shape of a shield. The silver was so polished it shone like a mirror. She unhooked the necklace and the bracelet and returned to the living room. She lifted the flap of the pouch, put some of her fingers inside and pulled out a key, a golden key with a special head welded onto it, a head with tiny words engraved on it. She read the words out loud, "Even death will not part us. Vivian, forget me not, at your peril." Whose key was it? What door would it open? All she knew now was that her name was Vivian and that it was related to the Spanish verb *vivir*, to live. Without knowing why, she knew she must leave the apartment and look for where the key would fit. An unknown force or instinct had then led her to the palace on the river.

Beauty Parade

As she sat in the lecture hall of the edifice Vivian wondered, once again, why she knew what she knew, why she saw what she saw. For instance, though the auditorium was empty, she could see dramas playing upon the stage. She could see all kinds of people, of all shapes, parading across the shiny surface.

There was the German baroness who pranced across in a crepe cloth stolen from a funeral home, her head shaved, lacquered a high vermillion. She led a duplicate baroness in spats and a tin can bra. She was a performance artist considered to be a daughter of the New York Dada Movement of the 1920's. Then atop a moving sled came the Cuban exile, or rather her life-size wooden copy. She was in flames, part of her already blackening. But if one looked closely at the face one could see that it was scarred from myriad facial cosmetic surgeries she had actually undergone in the 1970's. Her facial changes were considered, by her, as artistic, as her sculpture.

Then, also on a moving sled, came an enormous fish bowl with a man inside being tube-fed a liquid diet, apparently for a whole week. In the early 2000's, he'd been described as "marinated in unreality," as if dead, as if he'd been persecuted and killed by Roman guards of long ago. Many thought he was trying to top another artist who, in the 1970's, had his hands nailed to the roof of a Volkswagen.

Walking slowly, gracefully, a Russian woman around sixty years of age, followed. She was totally nude with a real human skeleton strapped onto her front. Sometimes she poked her face out—it was strangely decorated. The black design stretched from her chin to her forehead—it was a live scorpion.

Another moving sled appeared, this time with a man encaged in a box with bars that carried a sign, "Lived one year in this crate doing nothing."

And still from the early 2000's floated a lovely young woman in a wedding gown with a thumb out to indicate she was hitchhiking. Vivian knew she had hitchhiked from Italy to the Balkans, then to the Middle East. She saw herself as a messenger of peace, of togetherness. Vivian knew she ended up raped and strangled in Turkey.

No matter what had transpired in Vivian's past, of which she knew nothing, she did know she was not easily shocked. But the next participant in the parade totally floored her. She turned away in disgust as she saw the image of Hitler strutting across the stage in an immaculate crisp uniform, his hair and moustache carefully oiled in place, his back and limbs straight and rigid as if braced against a blast of wind, not wanting to look weak or scared. He was dragging what looked like a partially decomposed corpse labeled "Hitler and Europe in the name of his Brutal Father."

Then the stage lights were extinguished. Silence. Vivian was relieved. She thought the show as over. But as she rose to leave, a drumbeat began from the stage area and its lights came on again. Vivian knew the worse was yet to come, if that was possible after the atrocities she had seen as humanity sorted itself out between birth and death, between consciousness and oblivion. They appeared, a string of smiling men and women on crutches. They were missing a leg. They were followed by wheelchairs with people missing both legs. Afterwards there followed sprightly dancing forms with no arms, or only one arm. Vivian would not have been surprised to see a four-limbed person with no head doing cartwheels across the stage. An announcer hidden from view declared that these performers were all content, at peace. They had received the surgery that they had craved for so long, the amputation of a limb, despite the fact the limb was healthy. Now they felt whole at last, beautiful. All was well. The beauty parade could come to an end.

Vivian walked out into the hall in a daze, looking down to make sure her legs were still there. The only thing she was missing was her memory, her past, her identity. Who knows, maybe she wasn't even human. Maybe she was some kind of a puppet. She walked over to the window and looked at the river. It was already dusk. The river rippled soundlessly as the cars on the highway next to it roared along, red lights on one lane as they headed north, and white lights on the other side as they headed south. She caressed first one arm and then the other. Returning to lean against the wall she closed her eyes. She felt black and blue all over as if she'd been punched over and over again. When she reopened her eyes there was Roland in his wheelchair. She had forgotten their encounter of a few weeks back. She realized she hadn't seen him roaming the halls. She couldn't believe what she saw.

"My God, Roland, where are your legs?"

"I didn't want them," he answered calmly.

"What!" Vivian was aghast. "Are you crazy?"

"They were no good to me. I had never wanted them ever since I was a child. Then they just stopped functioning as if they knew they weren't wanted, that they weren't appreciated, loved."

Vivian persisted, "How could you hate them? They were yours. They were full of life—they made it possible for you to run, skip, twirl, leap into the air."

"I felt I shouldn't have them. They were foreign, somehow, intruders who didn't belong—there was something malevolent about them," Roland answered matter-of-factly.

"That's so strange. How on earth did you come to think like that? As if your very own legs were an enemy, a dangerous enemy!"

"Vivian, see, I remember your name," he smiled broadly. "Listen, I can't answer your questions. All I know is that now I am without fear. I am pure, free, able to fly as I wish, with no one hanging over me or under me, ready to punish me, perhaps even killing me."

"How did you get anyone to do the surgery?"

"Easy! I developed a fast-moving deadly infection.

They did it to save my life." And laughing merrily Roland wheeled himself away.

Mannequins in the Window

Vivian sat in the circle of chairs with the other patients as they awaited the guest speaker, a sex therapist, Dr. Frederick Manning. As she looked around her she saw that the edifice had been aptly named, a long time ago, Hospital for the Ruptured and Maimed. Its new name was so mediocre she had a hard time remembering what it was.

Seated near her was Francine with the round blue eyes, blond curls, perfectly aligned white teeth. She waddled around, her rounded short arms moving like flippers, tiny crooked fingers at the very ends. Mark always wore enormous fur gloves and fur earmuffs that made his emaciated body seem even smaller. The elegant middle-aged woman Nuala walked like an American Indian Warrior, tall, straight, her feet hardly touching the ground, her teeth clenched, the black cane held closely by one side, hidden in the folds of her black garments. There were maybe six others who were like mirror images of each other, swollen looking, overwhelming their wheelchairs, or so angular and gray they blended in with their walkers.

Vivian wondered why no one had questioned her presence, but then she might look more maimed than she knew. Though she looked into the full-length mirror in her shabby apartment, from time to time, the light was so bad she wasn't certain what she looked like. The only aspect of herself she paid attention to was her hair. But why was it she needed to wax the ends, to spike it outwards? Why did she need to look other-worldly, ageless, genderless, a little like a winged being? She'd recently noticed she had no penis, no vestiges of any, not even a small one. She knew from her bowel and urinating movements that she must have two openings; she could find no others. So, with no memory, in addition, she too was ruptured but how would she know this, how would she know what the norm was? How would the others know what was under her hieroglyphic clothes? Roland at first had almost wheeled right through her, the painter of grotesqueries had taken her for granted, the sisters looked at her as if she were a ghoul, and Kivi referred to her coming out of a costume party. But all had basically accepted her as belonging there with them, as one of them, part of them. They hadn't called security or a nurse.

Still sitting in the circle, waiting, Vivian wondered what they were all expecting from the meetings with a variety of specialists: physical therapists, dance therapists, social workers offering relaxation and visualization exercises, occupational experts with their display of helpful gadgets from canes, reachers to long shoehorns, and medical researchers with all the current news on new medications, new hopes for cures of all the rheumatic diseases. Though she herself did not have a chronic physical illness, she felt as if she did. Deep down she felt pain, discomfort, a sense of desperation, a wish for relief to be given to her by all the specialists. Nuala was the only one who thought that they themselves were responsible for their dis-ease by being who they were. She was the only one who thought they had to change themselves in order to get better.

Finally, Frederick appeared with his wife Helga who was also a sex therapist. They were both tall, big-boned, he with a full beard, looking like Rasputin, the charismatic Russian priest from history. Helga had a crew cut and eyes that smiled even when her lips didn't move.

As soon as they joined the circle Frederick plunged right in with a question, "How many of you are having sex? Raise your hand." No one responded, except to look at each other with disbelief.

"Okay, so maybe you're not able to copulate in the traditional fashion—how many of you are having any kind of sex, petting, kissing?" Again no one raised their hand, this time not even moving.

"I thought so. Now, don't be shocked, we're all human, how many of you fondle yourselves?" Not a sound in the room.

Vivian stood up abruptly, "Come on, is this necessary? This is too sudden. Some of us don't even know who we are, our own bodies, where we begin and where we end. For some of us it's as if we're just born." Many nodded.

Vivian continued, "Our illness erases us and yet, in a weird way, it also gives us a new life, a chance of a new beginning."

"What do you suggest?" Frederick smiled, perhaps from discomfort.

"Well," Vivian began, "How do babies learn about their bodies, how do they learn to walk, how do they learn about love, about pleasure?"

Helga responded this time, "Yes, I think I understand. We must begin at the beginning, we need to start all over again. Let us get together next week. By then, Rick and I will have put together a new program."

Surprisingly enough all of them showed up the following week. The room was set up differently—no chairs, a padded elevated platform in the middle. They started out sitting on the edge. Then they were asked to scoot backwards till their legs were also up and then they were to lay back. Rick and Helga stood up on the platform helping those that needed a push or a pull. When everyone was flat on their backs with their legs as straight as possible, though most often they were bent at the knee, their backs arched, their feet curled inwards, the couple sat down cross-legged in the middle.

Over several sessions they kicked their legs aimlessly, thrashed their arms around and giggled endlessly, all the while being praised by Rick and Helga. Then they crawled around any way they could. Unable to get on their afflicted knees, many just slithered on one side or on their behinds. Others rocked in one place as if about to plunge forward. A few merely sat up and imagined they were crawling rapidly on all fours, laughing mischievously. Rick and Helga bent down and hugged all of them.

Finally, one by one, each was helped to their feet, held up and guided by the leaders to a mirror where they were to admire themselves from eye to toe. Held upright from behind each traced their outline with their fingers, saying, "I like myself." The group chanted, "We like you too."

Vivian could see that Francine was enthralled by the exercises—her flipper-like arms and waddle did not impede her—she was stroked and praised for all her movements. Mark looked like a furry caterpillar with his gloves and earflaps, creeping in ecstasy, arching his thin long back when complimented. Nuala floated like a graceful log on a river, her erect posture unchanging. To Vivian some of the others were like embryos or stillborns, unable to navigate, not heeding the others around them. She herself felt as if she came from another world, not understanding what was expected of her. At first she lay still on her back seeing herself as a white silky beached whale without consciousness. Then she saw herself as a prehistoric baby mammoth being excavated from the snow by proud archaeologists exclaiming all the while about the perfection of the state of preservation in which they had found her. Later as she had kicked, thrashed about she felt she was coming out of a deep coma, wanting only to tear out all the tubes that invaded her. As she stood in front of the well-lit mirror, unassisted, she thought she saw a humanized bat deity with ears, hair forming a halo of sorts, her winged arms holding her up like crutches. She was not a regular person. She'd been born out of some calamity, a traumatic illness that had affected her body and mind, her very brain, her memory, her identity. But who had left her in that coffin of an apartment? Who had given her the golden key? Who had engraved upon it the words, "Even death will not part us. Vivian, forget me not, at your peril?"

Now on the sixth and last session as she once again sat in the circle, she wondered, who it was she mustn't forget. She looked around her. The people in the edifice were the only ones she knew, beginning with Roland, then the artist, followed by the two sisters, Kivi and the delimbed of the stage show.

Rick was asking, "So, have you done your homework, touched all of yourselves while looking into the mirror?"

Some smiled coyly, some were stony-faced, others were simply bewildered. Vivian raised her hand. Rick was relieved as he said, "Oh, good!" to Vivian.

"I did the exercise but I don't know what I felt because I wasn't there. It was as if I was the 'other' touching another 'other.'" Everyone laughed heartily looking triumphantly or mockingly at Rick and Helga.

"Where did you go, if you weren't there?" Helga inquired quietly.

"I was hiding somewhere. I didn't like the world I was in."

"What didn't you like about the world?"

"I don't know—maybe that I wasn't there?"

Again everyone laughed. "I'm sorry," Vivian continued, "I am not being flippant. It's just that all I see is pain, meanness, fear, nothingness. I don't *feel* who I am. I see an image in the mirror but I just *feel* a bloated blob bobbing around in the ocean, no arms, legs, no head, just little eyes, a gaping hungry mouth."

"How sad for you!" Helga exclaimed, "But why hide, why not fight, why not try to change the world, change yourself, disguise yourself, recreate yourself?"

"I don't know. It's as if I had no choice, as if I was being hunted, haunted," Vivian almost moaned. "As if I belong to someone else, were part of another. I think I chose to die but I didn't, so here I am."

Everyone looked at Vivian with sympathy, pity, shaking their heads, wrinkling their brows, making small sounds like, "Shhhh, shhhh." Perhaps they were attempting to soothe her, to shush her into quietude.

Yes, Vivian thought, that's what the world had been telling her, "Hush, hush, silence!"

Rick sighed deeply. He turned away from Vivian saying, "Does anyone else want to share what thoughts or feelings they had when touching themselves?"

Nuala spoke, "I felt nothing. All of my body had the same sensation as my elbow."

"Well, that's a good beginning—an elbow has the capacity of much feeling, electrical far-reaching waves," Rick almost mumbled.

Mark exclaimed, "My furry hands upon my body were very warming like hibernating against my mother's belly in a dark cave."

"Good, good!" But neither Rick or Helga looked pleased. They glanced at each other like trapped creatures.

Suddenly Vivian felt what Rick and Helga may have been feeling. She was horrified—what was wrong with her, with all of them? Where had their passions gone—love, hopes, dreams, appetites? Why were they virtually comatose? Perhaps it was themselves they had forsaken, forgotten—their very souls. Surely it wasn't illness that was to blame. Could it be that illness was only the result?

Sucking at the Jugular

Vivian glided right into the meeting with Nuala, holding her by the elbow as if she were her companion-caretaker. She sat meekly in a corner while everyone else took their seats around a long table. It was a meeting of the Community Advisory Board. The windows overlooked the river. Every time Vivian saw a seagull she was reminded of Roland. She wondered how he was doing without his legs. Perhaps she had lost her memory, her past, because it was as abhorrent to her as Roland's legs were to him.

Dr. Harkness, the Physician-in-Chief, began the meeting, "I want to introduce today's guest Nuala Branch. She is a patient-advocate and will be presenting a short paper on what she sees as a need for a self-help group for rheumatic disease patients." There was a collective sigh on the part of the five physicians, two rheumatologists, two research scientists and one orthopedic surgeon.

Nuala picked up her notes off the table with trembling hands, her fingers long, slender, but swollen and red at the joints. Her voice quavered a little but it was as twinkly as a schoolgirl's though she was in her thirties. "I am now in the process of being trained as a facilitator of a self-help mutual aid group at the New York Self-Help Clearinghouse of the City University. The aim of this group on these premises would be to learn to help ourselves and others like us without a professional overseer. Obviously, it would consist only of patients run by patients. Basically this group would be a workshop wherein we would seek ways of dealing with our specific concerns with those who share the same problems." Several more long sighs were heard as Nuala continued with Dr. Harkness looking from one doctor to another with admonishing frowns and nods. "The reason we need such an exclusive group is subtle. As you know, when a person becomes chronically ill he regresses emotionally. However, he is still an adult with the right to be respected as an adult. Therefore, it is not advisable to have to totally depend on the physician for his well-being since the doctor is a parent-like figure. This dependence is childlike and could lead to painful humiliations, disappointments and disillusionments." Vivian shuddered uttering a small "oh!" that only Nuala heard.

"Are you implying," Dr. Orski, the surgeon laughed, "that we have it in us to be the bad guy, the villain?"

Dr. Harkness responded sharply, "Come on Bob, let Ms. Branch finish her thoughts."

Nuala looked around her, at everyone's face, but avoided Dr. Orski's. She had noticed his gruff look of disdain from the very beginning. "We, as patients, are aware that we need to understand ourselves better, how we interrelate with our diseases, how our lives are impacted and changed. We need to find ways to become more responsible for our own fate. We need to educate ourselves, to gain more coping tools. We need to find ways to better express ourselves so we can be more of a partner to our health specialists. We can't continue as poor victims waiting to be rescued by heroes. Thank you for listening."

Before Dr. Harkness could invite questions or comments, Dr. Orski's voice boomed out, "Your little group sounds more like a mutual commiseration society where all of you run off in a huff to lick your wounds!"

Nuala suddenly looked at him fully in the face, her hazel-green eyes flashing with energy, her small mouth becoming twisted, "What makes you think that? You sound like someone who's been rejected, or are you feeling guilty for not healing us!"

Dr. Penn, one of the rheumatologists, stepped in, "Now, now," he laughed, "Of course it's nothing like that but perhaps it would be more time and cost effective if all of us concentrated on inspiring patients to be more compliant, listening to instructions, taking their medications, not being so combative."

Nuala answered with a tiny sigh of impatience, "As I mentioned before, illness regresses us. Maybe some of us were infantile to begin with—after all we have the same personality problems as the rest of the world, but, in any case, we need to feel less helpless."

Dr. Orski cut in gruffly, "Okay, so maybe we can make more education available to you through our nurses and social workers, but you certainly shouldn't just go off by yourselves."

Nuala continued, frowning, "Maybe our diseases are wakeup calls alerting us that we must make a move to change ourselves. To do this we need our own space in which to experiment. This doesn't mean we're divorcing our doctors. We still love you, after all, till death do us part!"

Vivian jumped a little in her seat, startled by the mention of the marital vow. What was it her key said? "Not even death will part us." Once again she considered from whom this message could have come from. Her instincts told her that it must be from someone more powerful than a husband, or a doctor. Could it be from a deity, a demon, an unseen force?

One of the researchers spoke hesitantly, "I'm very disappointed, I sense so much resentment in you Ms. Branch. Our physicians have done so much work on you, reconstructions, replacements. You're not bedridden as a result. You're ambulatory."

Nuala snapped, "You think I'm an ingrate, I'm not." But, frankly, your reaction makes me feel belittled as if I've been a bad girl. Don't you see, we need to grow up without mama and papa watching us, judging us or simply protecting us, making it clear they're sacrificing so much for us. You are all inherently generous—if you could, you'd walk, run, leap for us, so that we didn't have to struggle, to suffer."

Many took deep breaths, but didn't speak. Even Dr. Harkness seemed to be waiting for something. Vivian stood up abruptly, her arms expanding sideways as if unfurling her wings. She fixed her beady black eyes and her glittering bracelet upon everyone, one at a time. Her voice was more like a hum, a vibration, "Forgive me, I'm new here. I came with Nuala. I'm a volunteer patient-helper."

Dr. Harkness beamed, not disturbed by the intrusion, "No, no, you're most welcome young woman, you look like someone who has something to say."

"Well, in my travels around this esteemed building I've heard many things, surprising things." Everyone stared at her as she continued, "I heard one of your physicians say that doctors needed a support group because all the rheumatic disease patients sucked at their jugular."

"What does that have to do with anything?" Dr. Orski grumbled.

"If you professionals need to support each other, to recuperate yourselves, in effect, why can't you understand patients needing the same. After all, their diseases are eating *them* up."

Dr. Orski stood up, pushing his chair roughly back with such force it fell over backwards, "I can't believe what I hear, what I see. What's this nonsense with the dramatics, the getup, that bracelet? Are we into witchcraft now after all our scientific advancements? We don't have time for this. We have work to do. Patients are waiting for us."

Nuala also stood up, slowly, painfully, leaning on her knuckles upon the table, "Please don't be disrespectful. Vivian is one of us. Perhaps we need to be outrageous, dramatic. We need to moan, grown, cry, play out our little dramas like children with costumes, with shiny things and we need to do this in our own playroom without nannies, teachers or parents. Surely you know that child's play is a dress rehearsal for living." Nuala sat down again with more agility than she'd expected.

"Sounds more like a kindergarten or a lunatic asylum." Dr. Orski muttered as he picked up his chair and flung himself into it.

Ignoring this comment, Dr. Penn spoke in a gentle voice, "I think we can agree that we certainly could get your group a room in the building where you can do whatever you want to your hearts' content. We won't interfere."

Nuala frowned, "I don't like the way you're saying that—you sound annoyed, sarcastic. Don't you understand, of course, we need a patient group but *only* as part of a whole program of treatment. The vision is to ultimately interact with all the pertinent health professionals."

Vivian added, "That's right. We don't want to be isolated. We don't want to go off to our own self-commiseration society as was mentioned earlier. We only want to be ourselves in the fullest sense, as we join in with you, in an equal way, to help us all to deal better with our illnesses."

Once again Dr. Orski stood up but this time in a slow dignified way, "By the way, who're you? You're not even a patient, are you?

"As I said before, I'm a volunteer patient-helper."

"Well, Ms. Whoever You Are, we don't appreciate strangers coming here to lord it over us, prancing around, like who knows what, alienating our patients."

"Doctor, in many ways you're right. I know how I must look and sound to you. I sometimes look that way to myself, too."

Dr. Orski laughed, "You're such a phony. What are you playing at, what's your game?"

"I'm trying to belong, to exist, to find the way."

"Well, Ms. Phony, go somewhere else, go back to where you came from. You don't belong here, in this room, in this establishment."

Dr. Harkness interceded, "Come, come, Bob, let's not be hasty. Ms. Vivian is Ms. Branch's companion, her helper, assistant. I've hard many positive things about her. Patients have told me she tells them stories, advises them. Yes, they find her strange but they like that she doesn't say the usual things, that she doesn't look conventional. She has a good effect on everyone. They feel better after they've been with her."

Nuala murmured, "Thank you, Dr. Harkness."

The doctor continued, "Let's take some time out to reconsider all that has been said, all that has happened. We'll meet in a month to once again discuss a patient-led group. Next time we'll invite a psychologist, a social worker, a nurse, a rehabilitation expert, maybe even a health journalist. We need more diversity in order to get more unison. Perhaps we all need to expand our vision."

Dr. Orski marched out ahead of everyone else muttering something inaudible while glancing at Vivian.

She thought he said, "Go to hell!"

For the first time since she was frightened by the pounding at the door, Vivian felt a deep sense of dread, as if someone wanted to skin her alive, to rip off her face as if it were a mask. What was worse was that she had no idea what was underneath.

Pandora's Curse

Nuala and Vivian went to a nearby pub for a bite and a drink. It was called *The Recovery Room.*

"Do you think I'm a phony?" Vivian asked as she slowly sipped her Bloody Mary with both a wedge of lime and one of lemon.

Nuala answered after gulping down half a glass of sparkling mineral water, "No, you're real, but odd real, not real, real."

"Well, Dr. Orski was right," Vivian whispered, I'm not for real. I don't even know who I am. I'm some kind of a fraudulent human, a counterfeit, an impostor. I don't even know where I came from, who made me, raised me. Suddenly I just was who I am." And Vivian told Nuala about her apartment, the key. She tried to be as succinct as possible but found herself talking hesitantly, almost stammering. She was confused—she wasn't sure she should even talk about her plight. There was something embarrassing about missing so much of herself, of seeing that she seemed to be made up of bits of this and that, piecemeal, a true phantom self, not there at all but thinking she is, like a phantom limb, not there, but felt as if it were there.

Nuala listened sympathetically, "You're like a Pandora, made by diverse deities, then delivered to this life, perhaps destined to reveal the secrets behind our maladies."

Vivian's small black eyes seemed to become larger, "You make it sound okay, logical somehow."

After Nuala ordered a vegetable burger and Vivian asked for a rare hamburger, Nuala continued, "I've always felt close to the dark side. I seem to have an affinity for the mysterious."

"So, Nuala, seriously, are *you* able to trace your own life from one incident to another, over the years, you know, are you able to find and recognize the blocks that make up the structure that is you?"

"Not really. I have deliberately forgotten large chunks of my life."

"How could you? I'd give anything to remember, no matter what—a memory of a life, any life, is so precious!"

Nuala fell silent, feeling criticized. After a few minutes Vivian asked, "So you've had many orthopedic surgeries, that must have been awful, no? You know, the healing, recovering and all that."

"Well, I must say, I should be a bionic woman but I'm not—just more mobile."

"Were the surgeries very painful?" Vivian persisted. "How did you manage the trauma of being cut up even if for your own good? What joints did you have worked on?"

"From my neck to my toes and believe it or not, I actually looked forward to the surgeries and *not* for the usual reasons of eventually becoming more mobile."

"Oh, what other reasons could there be?" Vivian began to feel apprehensive, inadvertently remembering the eerie beauty parade in the auditorium.

"Each extraction represented being rid of something bad within me, you know, as they say in psychology, a bad object, a negative nagging element was excised. The replacement would render me purified, renewed." Nuala sounded excited, almost ecstatic, as she continued. "Once while recovering from the anesthesia, I dreamt that I gave birth to myself, and for a moment, when I awoke, I thought my bandaged leg was my baby!"

"Dr. Orski would have loved to hear you talk this way!" Vivian laughed. "He would have branded you a witch for using surgery as a form of exorcism, surgery as a cure for being possessed, bewitched. But Nuala, doesn't it worry you that you *need* these operations, in effect, to reconstruct your invisible inner world?"

"Yes, it worries me, but only a little and only once in a while."

Vivian couldn't resist pursuing her thoughts, "Doesn't it worry you that maybe you developed your disease so your inner demons could become visible and therefore could be conquered, killed, banished?"

"My God, what a thought!" Nuala was horrified. She reached for Vivian's untouched glass of water and drank it all down to the last drop. Then she added, "I'm not a genie you know, able to dream things up and make them true. Anyway what a thing to do to myself since these autoimmune diseases take on a life of their own like many monsters of this world—Dr. Frankenstein's monster, Mr. Hyde, the portrait of Dorian Gray, atomic power and so forth and so on."

Laughing, Vivian called the waitress and ordered another Bloody Mary, a double this time. After a few sips she ventured, "By the way, do you have a hidden agenda for our group?"

"What do you mean?" Nuala was puzzled.

"Do you want us to learn something other than how to become more responsible, more individualistic?"

"Isn't that enough?" Nuala's voice rose a little. "Responsibility entails taking some of the blame for being ill, you know, not dealing well with our psychological traumas. Why just blame fate, karma, the environment, genetics, accidents, fly-by-night viruses, a weakened immune system?"

"It sounds a little critical, judgmental for me, bringing in the causes of disease and, forgive me, but perhaps bringing in your own hang-ups. Why not just deal with learning to cope well with diseases? Why not leave out the complexities of causes?" Vivian's voice was taking on a pleading tone.

"I know, *I* know how I must sound but by looking to ourselves and our own culpability we give ourselves power, freedom." Once again Nuala's voice began to rise in passion, "We can act as if we're truly separated from bad objects, bad inner influences, whether we are or not. We can act as if we can stand up straight within our own sensible snub-nosed shoes!" Nuala laughed so raucously people nearby turned around to look at the two women.

What a sight they must have made—one tall, lanky, all in black, long hair, no jewelry, black-framed eyeglasses, in her thirties; the other not as tall, not as slender, perhaps in her forties, looking like an immigrant from a far off rainforest. Neither seemed to have breasts or much of any buttocks. Neither had any gracefulness, fluidity of movement or signs of musicality in their voices.

"Changing the subject Nuala, what do you think happened to me, you know, aside from your Pandora story? Where do I go from here? I don't have a sense of being guided anymore, the way I was in the beginning, when I was pointed towards the hospital."

"Well, okay," Nuala began "let's look at all the clues on hand: You're not a youngster, so you've lived a life. You're not ignorant, you don't have a blank mind, so you've had an education. You have some refinement, delicacy, so you've been exposed to sophistication. However, your way of dressing, of doing your hair, your shoes, reminding us of bare feet, are a little alien. You have plenty of money. Your rent and utilities have been paid in advance for a long time, so someone was, or is, looking after you. Now, this 'someone' is either an enemy out to hurt you or he's a teacher who is testing you, teaching you a lesson, even going to the extent of causing your amnesia with drugs or to an even greater extent of causing a traumatic experience, psychological or medical that brought on the amnesia."

"So what! We know all this already, don't we?"

"I know, I know," Nuala muttered, "I'm just summarizing. Now to the nitty-gritty—who on earth would challenge you never to forget him? Who would threaten you with harm, with death? I hate to say this but it has to be someone who's bigger than life. It has to be either a real deity or a very good imitation.

"Can't be! You don't really believe that, do you?" Vivian exclaimed.

"Not really. So, it has to be someone who's an egomaniac, a very grandiose one at that! Perhaps a disappointed husband, a spurned lover, an abandoned father or mother, an undervalued physician?"

"Why not throw in a predatory priest, an evil magician and God knows who else?" Vivian lamented.

"I'm worry—I know I haven't been of much help," Nuala muttered.

Vivian was almost on the verge of crying, "Why do I have the feeling that I'm not too long for this life? There's no way I can keep going the way I am. Perhaps once I discover what the key signifies, what it opens or reveals, that will be it, the end, finito, finis, lo último. Perhaps this is all I'm here for: to live a life that is just a slow suicide, to martyr myself for God knows what reason, perhaps only to illustrate how *not* to live, how one *mustn't* forget how to live well, fully being oneself, relishing memories, reveling in whatever identify one has, without judgment."

"Are you frightened?" Nuala asked, not knowing what else to say.

"Not really. In a way I want it all to end. I don't like waiting. I had a dream the other night that I left the city and headed for the edge of the forest knowing that someone called Mufas was waiting for me."

"Sounds like 'move fast,' said rapidly, certainly not 'slow up and die,' Nuala whispered tenderly, placing a hand on Vivian's shoulder."

Phantasms

Sitting in her dark apartment waiting for the next day so she could go back to the hospital, Vivian looked through her red notebook. It seemed so long since she'd started sketching and writing in it. There was a drawing of the two beautiful young sisters arriving by ambulance, each looking aggrieved, bitter. She wondered where on earth the story came from, the one she told them in such detail, the fairytale of a princess who didn't know she was special, the fable about the evils of shedding blood, of being unkind to life.

Vivian's enormous bracelet lay facing her on the small table in front of her. The beaded necklace with the pouch containing the golden key also lay in front of her. As the room grew darker the bracelet grew brighter and brighter as if lit by an inner fire. She took the key out of the pouch and held it clasped in both hands on her lap. It felt hot but she didn't let go of it. It seemed to be sending waves of light into her heart, her head. The key itself seemed to be burrowing its way through her, looking for a place where it could lodge itself, where it could find a safe haven, the spot where it belonged.

No matter how much Vivian fought against losing

consciousness, losing control, she fell into a hypnotic state. She was transported to other places, rapidly moving from one small house to another on tree-lined streets. All the streets in every town, in every state of America had rows and rows of houses, all with green lawns and front porches. Many had a dog tied to a long rope, barking in the backyard. Everywhere people were wary of her. She knew why, she was a stranger from far off. Though this was his homeland they were wary of her husband also. Perhaps because he was so short, bald, shy, marching around as if in uniform, wearing all white clothes with a black belt and black loafers. People were wary of their two little girls as well. They were too well-behaved, working in the vegetable garden, weeding, watering, picking fruit, serious, looking like little old women in crisp aprons and bonnets, always wearing silk socks, probably hand-embroidered in some foreign place. In addition, they wore patent leather shoes that were always shiny. Later as they grew older, bigger, the girls wore plaid dresses with white lace collars and had ribboned long braids. They were always carrying schoolbooks or groceries, still serious, hardly ever smiling.

As Vivian continued in a trance, the scene changed abruptly. She saw herself fallen on the bathroom floor. She was unconscious, sprawled out in a pool of blood, her womb and ovaries eaten from within by raggedy lumps of cells. There was a rush to a hospital, immediate surgery. In time, who knows how long, she was sent home but with no medicine, no care. Her body and mind went into a turmoil—so much had changed in her organs, her glands, the working of the flow of her blood. She became disoriented, depressed. She began to feel deserted, helpless. She wandered around the neighborhood looking for her pet jaguars, her crocodiles, her jungle leaves and vines. She called out to the princess who didn't know she was special. Finally, her husband ended up in the arms of a more attentive woman. Her daughters looked at her as if she were a retardate who didn't care for anyone or anything. Even in her mesmerized state Vivian questioned herself. Was she seeing her life, her past? Had she lost her memory and disappeared? Had she herself rented that dark apartment, changed her appearance, her attire, obtained those few trinkets she had, even had the key engraved?

The key became cold in her hands. The bracelet stopped glowing. Vivian went to bed though she dreaded the bedroom, usually trying to avoid it by sleeping curled up on the sofa in the living room. But now that she was beginning to know herself, her past, she was dead tired needing to stretch out. Lying on the clammy sheets with her eyes tightly closed, she could still see the shadows on the wall, branches, leaves, drops of rain, swaying, rising and falling. She could hear the droplets of water quietly knocking at the window, the only one not boarded up by her, as if she'd wanted some evidence of there being an outside life despite her wishes to become interred within the dark tomb of the apartment. She knew she had wished to be dead but that she hated to see blood. She needed to find a clean way to die without shedding blood, without feeling it throbbing around her neck, without sensing it screeching to a stop. Blood had gained a form, a presence. It was a monster haunting her, hunting her down. It was a demon she had to avoid. How else could she die, then? Of course, that's why she headed for the hospital, the one for the ruptured and the maimed. It was in a hospital she'd lost everything. Perhaps she could find herself in another hospital.

But before finally falling into a deep sleep, Vivian asked herself, why did she write that message on the key, why so pompous, grandiose? Were Una and Tess really her daughters, if so, should she re-enter their lives? Why? They didn't need each other. Each had to find her own way through life. She was the same person of long ago and yet she was not. Whatever had changed made her different. Vivian was no longer the jungle girl, the princess, the lover of warriors, the mother of dead sons, the begetter of alienated daughters.

During that deep sleep Vivian had a dream she would never remember. She didn't need to. It was just another adventure to experience, to feel. She dreamt of herself in several parts. First, she's standing in a large foyer and hears a thud in the nearby kitchen. She knows instantly that she'd stabbed someone to death. She's afraid the murderer will be coming for her next. Second, she runs upstairs with her replica right behind her with arms extended towards her, long fingers with dagger-like nails. She rushes into an empty room and heads for the open window. Third, looking out over the fields and the forest beyond, she sees herself galloping away on a horse towards the tall trees. She turns as the villain approaches her, slowly seeming to be transforming itself. Fourth, before long there in front of Vivian stood a giant golden key, still menacing but without the arms, the fingers, the nails, without any weapons. It advanced towards her, slowly, elegantly, regally. Vivian was paralyzed with terror, blinded by the golden fire. Fainting, she began to fall. The key entered her like the shaft of light in a medieval painting of Santa Teresa, filling her with the melted gold.

When Vivian awakened the sheets were no longer clammy. They were hot as if pressed by a hot iron. She was suffused by a vibrancy in every nerve, every cell of her body. She felt so different but remembered nothing of the night. However, she knew with a keen certitude that she was not invisible. She was no longer haunted, hunted. She was no longer afraid, not needing to disappear, to run away. She felt whole, not splintered. She was her very soul, herself in every way. Whether she knew it or not the golden key had found out where it fit, what it unlocked. It had found out where it belonged.

THE SAGA OF THALASSA AND LARANA: A LOVE STORY

Beneath the Swirling Waters

She's a type of a witch because her dreams appeared real and reality only a dream. Strangely enough we find our witch in bed, in a hospital that overlooked an estuary that looked like a river. She couldn't walk. She had suddenly lost the use of her legs and was bedridden. All she could do was wait for a diagnosis and treatment.

She had the impression that the glimmering waters awaited her every night. She knew she could swim. So she'd find an open window and slither down the halls and walls into the water. Once submerged she began her search for a special spot where she imagined the two opposing currents briefly came together, blending together ever so gently even though each was headed in their own direction.

One evening she saw a figure diving in and out of the whirlpool the currents were creating. He must have sprung out of the depths under her, in the darkest part of the river. Maybe he had emerged from a garden of flowers and weeds. The figure was that of a man, long, lean, strands of dark hair winding themselves around his pale face. His features looked as if they'd been carved in ivory in a far off land, sunken eyes, prominent cheekbones, a large mouth that could easily form itself into a smile that was not a smile. He was not a jocular figure but there was something about him that entranced her. He, on the other hand, did not like to be intruded upon, especially by a witch. He knew she was a witch because of the effect she had on him; he could feel her calling out to him; he could feel her silent demands; he was being enthralled by her love, her passion for him.

His groin was a garden itself containing a silky tubular stalk which floated happily by itself away from his master. Finally, when the stalk became tired it came quietly to rest upon the fruits of the man's body. She swam after him wanting to hold the long silkiness in her hands, protecting it as she caressed it. But he constantly eluded her with the help of myriads of ripples and waves.

Perhaps she'd lost the use of her legs because she had disowned them, finding them imperfect or perhaps she had sacrificed her legs so as to come to know the river, to meet the figure who was so at peace—he knew the pattern of his life—it was clear and constant. In all her sixty years of life she'd feared forces that opposed each other, such as the two currents where her beloved lived. He merely swam from current-to-current with great ease.

Though he'd mainly ignored her, eventually he began to study the intruder who had entered his peaceful domain. He wouldn't have wanted to know anything about her experiences on land. He wouldn't have understood how she'd so often been taunted by fears involving the unity and disunity within her relationships.

Well, it's time to give her a name. It was Larana because she leapt from one lily pad to another like a frog. Also perhaps she was aptly named because deep within her she sought to be exquisitely loved and be transformed into a regal joyous being, a deity steeped in the perfect balance of all contradictions.

One day, while still in the hospital, waiting for a diagnosis and treatment, Larana changed. She lost track of who she was and where she was. Everyone became an enemy. In one instance, she thought she'd been kidnapped and taken to another building. In another, a redheaded young man spied under her covers at dawn, the rising sun seeming to set his hair on fire. Then there was the bald man with too many teeth who pushed a tube through one nostril down to her stomach as he scolded her saying that this was what happened when someone refused to eat. Another time someone put her in a moving coffin saying they needed to see inside her legs. She was tortured by needles and by enormous pills needing to be swallowed. She was tormented by beds that folded her up or stretched her apart. Pans with hard edges were placed under her buttocks while being told to expel all the poisons inside her. White powders flew around her, suffocating her after she was scraped with a hot cloth. One night she was almost strangled when she was caught in the grip of myriads of cold cards hanging from above on what looked like scrawny metal trees with no leaves. One of the worse attacks came from a catheter that had gotten twisted, crushing some nerves that caused her spasms of agony.

Larana decided she must get back into the river. She planned never to return to the hospital. She would drown herself near her beloved. Maybe she could manage to choke on the waters in the spot where she thought the currents blended together. She wondered why it was that life eluded her instead of presenting her with a clear experience of energizing events.

As she began to think of the experiences in her life, she slithered even faster down the wall, eager to disappear once and for all. If only she could first embrace the figure, the man surrounded by a peaceful sameness. Her body lit up with the power of her yearning. Already part of her filled up with a pool of her own. But she wasn't able to enjoy the pleasure suffusing her body. She began to remember some of her experiences, the ones that split her in two, harassing her with their indecisiveness, their contradictions.

When did the two currents in her life begin to show themselves? It could be one evening when she was on the way upstairs feeling loved and secure. She was sixteen years old. Her father whom she adored stopped her saying he needed to tell her something that was always troubling him.

He had once loved a man. Nothing came of it—he was rejected. He swore he never again craved a man. Her father looked so vulnerable, so small, so pitiable. She didn't like that he looked this way. She didn't like that he had secrets—what else had he hid from her? Suddenly he seemed to become another person, not the strong man she relied upon to love her. It was then that she detached herself, wrenched away. It was then she realized each had been in their own current. She felt totally alone, deserted but she hadn't understood this at the time—she thought she was just jealous and confused because of the homosexual aspects of his revelation. She hadn't understood that what mattered, the only thing of real value, was that her father was a human being struggling to be loved. He floundered around in his own swirling current always wanting to merge with another. That's why he had always reached out to her, totally captivating her, making her part of himself.

During her first marriage, a year later, when she was seventeen, her father-in-law pronounced many times that everyone should live only to forty. Falling in love with Larana returned youthfulness to him. Desperately wanting the connection with someone, she led him on, only to reject him in the end, leaving her feeling guilty, torn in two and alone. So much so that once when out on a walk across Manhattan, she ended up being lured into a foyer by a stranger who requested very politely, shyly that she stand on his chest. As he lay on the tiled floor, she climbed on top of him holding onto the banister of the stairway. And when he further suggested she move her feet around on his soft but muscular chest, she complied. There was something about his face that touched her—he seemed so vulnerable, so tormented. What on earth had happened in his life to want so badly to be hurt, to be tormented? What could cause a person to split off from his soul, from humanity? And why was it possible for her, then eighteen or nineteen, to join the dance into hell and yet be able to be a lovely, lovable student with intelligence and wisdom?

Obviously, Larana couldn't accept the fact that something was wrong with her. Perhaps because it might mean that her connection to her father was spurious and not based on love, only the semblance of love. What was wrong was that she was nothing without his spirit being forever connected with her deep inside.

It's no wonder she fainted at a psychology lecture where real patients were presented and asked to discuss their problems. She fainted when the presenter, an ex-priest told of his sexual escapades with boys at night and his fervent priestly activities during the day. He was the perfect example of the split that rendered his need for connections an evil endeavor.

Then there was her long second marriage where somehow she sometimes managed to convey the impression she was a cheater and a liar. Unconsciously she painted a picture of evil doings that, in reality, did not exist.

• • •

Larana went straight to the special spot where the two currents merged together, but as hard as she tried she couldn't find it. She looked for her beloved and he was nowhere. Even the garden had disappeared. There was nothing around her but water that swirled in every direction. She let the water enter her nostrils and mouth but nothing happened. She couldn't even drown herself. All that was left was for her to leave the river. She now was forced to face the fact that she had to regain the use of her legs. She must learn to walk. She must accept her legs as her very own with all their imperfections. She must learn not only to nurture her legs but also to nurture her whole body, her self, her soul.

The Beckoning

One day Larana woke up in the recovery room to discover she had lost both of her knee prosthetics to a rampant infection.

"Let me die, I don't want to live!" she screamed at her doctors. "Oh, if only I could have drowned myself!"

One night, back in her room as she slept fitfully under the influence of heavy medications, she sensed a presence in her room. With difficulty she opened her eyes and there before her stood the figure from the garden deep down in the river, the river that flowed down below her hospital window. His dark hair was wet, separated into thick luxurious strands. He was naked except for a loincloth woven from heart-shaped leaves, upside down hearts. His eyes were blacker than ever as they pierced into her flesh seeming to be looking for her very core, beyond her maimed legs, her atrophied muscles, beyond all of her inner organs, beyond all the wildly circulating blood.

"I must be dreaming," she murmured, raising her head up, her brown hair springing up from behind her head, forming a spiky halo.

"No, you're not. I am real," he responded. "You are

the one who has drawn me away from my peaceful abode. Peaceful, despite the swirling currents."

"I didn't call you!" She was annoyed, bitter, not remembering how much he had impressed her before.

"I didn't call you," she repeated, "What makes you think I did?"

In a soft melodious voice he murmured, "I can feel the thoughts within you, even the ones you're afraid to reveal."

She became angrier, "Why should you care what I'm thinking or feeling! Is this some kind of a test, a game with which to amuse yourself?"

"I am from a special place from which all of life sprang. I belong to a different kind of human being. It is our responsibility to understand you, to help you," his voice had become even more musical.

Larana let her head drop back down on the bed as she raised the head of her bed mechanically by pressing a button.

"So why did you run from me when I swam after you? Not that I care anymore—I'm just an old cripple."

Sighing he answered, "Sometimes our responsibilities weigh too heavily on us and we try to avoid them. But I must heed that you need me, just as much as when you saw me the first time—don't deny it!"

Casting her eyes downward Larana almost whispered, "It was different then—I had only lost the use of my legs; I thought that if I so wished, I could regain control over them. Now whether I choose to or not I'll probably never walk again. I'm nothing, a non-being!" She closed her eyes. Then suddenly opening them she asked, "By the way, what is your name?"

"Thalassa," he pronounced loudly.

"How strange—that's Greek for the sea, no?"

"Yes, the sea that becomes rivers, lagoons, ponds, creeks. The sea where many creatures live. The ponds where frogs live, their eyes popping out, croaking in fear as well as in happiness. In Spanish they are called ranas. You should know—you're Larana, the frog."

"I can't help what I was named, "she was embarrassed.

Thalassa only smiled, always looking deeply into her whole being. She trembled, shivers crisscrossing her body as she asked, "You see yourself as my savior, my gallant savior?"

"Not really. Remember that it was the strength of your calling to me that brought me to you." He approached the bed and placed one of his hands on her chest, her breast, her heart. Once again she trembled. Soon spasms shook her from head to toe. She moaned, not understanding why she should be feeling such an energy enveloping her. She closed her eyes in order to feel more sharply. When she opened her eyes he was gone.

The next night he appeared before her again. She scolded, "I fear you'll be forever escaping from me, leaving me, hiding somewhere, not far away."

Thalassa laughed, "I don't have to be with you to be there by your side."

This time she looked piercingly at him, "I'm feeling sicker and sicker every time you leave me. I feel healed when you are with me even though I have no knees to walk with."

He approached her, taking her hand and placing it between his two hands, "You must learn to retain the substance of another in their absence. You must learn, now that you are older and wiser, to expel all that is not good for you."

Larana was puzzled, her broad forehead crinkling, her delicate nostrils tightening together, "What makes you say that to me?"

Thalassa merely continued, "Examine your past and practice with those you knew long ago, who was good for your vitality and who drank of your blood." He caressed her hair, patting it down. Then he bent down and softly kissed her cheeks. Again she trembled at his touch. Again she wanted to embrace him, to hold his maleness in her hands. But he slowly detached himself and backed out of the room, keeping his eyes in hers, fervently holding on, eye to eye. An embrace of sorts. She almost swooned.

She began looking back as he had suggested. She began remembering what was impossible to remember—when she was a baby. Her mother banished her to a crib after a whole year of sleeping with her. After other similar sudden rejections, Larana banished her mother from her heart, but her mother clung to her mind, sometimes disguising herself as a man, like her internist, little, plump, dark nurturing. She fell in love with him while at the same time pushing him away with an impervious disdain. But why was she holding onto her mother's ghost? Thalassa would say she had the power to let go, to let her mother waft away into oblivion.

She remembered when she was seventeen she had left home and was working at a children's camp. Her father called her on the phone to tell her he and the family were moving overseas. He was distressed, he sobbed loudly but she was not moved. She was devastated. She hung up on him, running into the woods of Vermont, climbing the steepest hills, crashing into tree branches, falling upon rocks, she cried, screaming out loud, wailing like a child as she bruised herself over and over again. But as she destroyed part of herself, she kept him vivid, undamaged in her mind, a yearning forever entrenched.

As her room grew darker and darker, the sun slowly setting, she waited for the streetlights to become reflected upon the rippling river. She almost sang in a low monotone, "Thalassa, Thalassa, love me with all of you just once, encompass all of me in one turbulent embrace and then I will be able to let you go. Will I be able to let you go or will I add you to my cracked urn of lost beings?" Her knees gone she would no longer be able to kneel before the urn hoping her lost loves would return to her. Would she ever be able to see them for what they were—blackened decomposed skeletons bearing no resemblance to love, to life? She must do what the doctors recommended, have prosthetic knees inserted into her legs, prosthetics made for walking not for kneeling. Why is it that in a way she'd rather die than go through the struggle of standing up on her own two legs? Would she also be willing to live with one or two amputations instead of disconnecting herself from murderous ghosts? Later that evening Thalassa screamed at her, "You are so selfish, self-centered. Your legs don't just belong to you. They belong to me, to the physicians, to all who care for you! If I were a believer, I'd say your limbs belong to God, to the Universe!" Larana almost sprang out of bed, her hair more pointed, more spiky than ever.

"No, no, no, they belong to me alone! I can do what I want with them! You have no right to badger me into compliance, into some kind of an ethical stance wherein I'm not free, wherein I must think of all of you. Oh why wasn't I able to drown myself as I wanted, as I wished!

Thalassa's eyes burned fiercely. "You couldn't because you are tied to others who wish for you to thrive."

Her eyes also inflamed she retorted, "Well, in that case, make love to me, connect with me, tear me apart and put me together again with passion, the passion of life. Larana tore off her hospital gown. She tore out the stomach tube inserted for force-feeding. Her face was flushed, sweaty, her eyes as glittering as the river.

Coming ever nearer to her bed, Thalassa said, "I want to do just that even though my people do not permit it. I may be forever banished from all waterways."

Larana reached for him, tearing off his loincloth of leaves. He was totally erect, glistening, ruddy, throbbing. As he backed away she continued, "Can't you just make love to me once, right now? Transform me into a vibrant being, a deity of love, from a mere frog to regality!"

"You know the answer, the only answer there can be." And Thalassa was gone.

Later that same night Larana escaped out of the building, slithering all the way into the river. She was determined to tie herself to the bottom, in the garden, tied by strong vines, remaining there to wilt or to drown. He was waiting for her in the garden, arms outstretched, no loincloth, erect, beckoning her to come to him. The strong currents pushed her towards him, her body palpitating with desire. Suddenly she began to choke, she couldn't breathe. "No, no!" she tried to shout as she reached for Thalassa. Water rushed into her mouth, her nose. She knew she was drowning at last. Had she gotten her wish or was life playing a joke on her? "No, no!" she shouted within herself as she swam upward towards the air. She didn't even look backwards at Thalassa, the love of her life.

Rupture

As Larana rose to her feet, a loud popping sound seemed to come from nowhere. She sat down again. She couldn't believe it but one of her legs felt frozen—it wouldn't obey her. She laughed while her lunch companion looked worried. No matter how much she tried to straighten the rogue leg, it wouldn't budge. Laughing once again she reached for her empty cup of sake. Calling the waiter, smiling coquettishly, she ordered another large vessel of the potent rice wine. After several gulps she tried once again to force her limb into compliance. It still wouldn't move. She realized she was lame.

• • •

Before the popping sound, before it was time to leave the Japanese restaurant, her friend had been telling her about his travels, his easy adaptation to new places, no matter how exotic, strange or primitive. Though Larana loved to travel, to see new sights, to experience interesting adventures, she always felt a sharp anguish in her heart when she was far away from her familiar surroundings, a home sickness, even a love sickness.

Paul leaned forward, pushing away his plate of tempura shrimp, his narrow frame seeming to become crunched, "Why do you think you feel this way?"

Larana sipped her sake, "I don't know but it's definitely some kind of neurosis."

"I'm surprised with all the traveling you did with your family when growing up."

Larana persisted, "I know, I shouldn't feel a lot of things but once when my father was overseas, World War II of course, my mother had just rented a house with beautiful shiny floors and I couldn't contain my unhappiness, my frustration, so I skated all over the house, on all the gleaming polished floors, leaving black streaks, lines and circles all made by my rubber soles."

"Maybe it had more to do with your father's absence than with the change, with moving," Paul continued looking deep into her eyes, following all the lines and ripples of her worn pained face.

Larana sighed, looking down, speaking only after many moments, "Who knows! All I know is that when he died at sixty-two, just a bit older than I am now," Larana paused, "Anyway I was in my late twenties, I had an enormous nervous breakdown which entailed running downhill, falling down, breaking an elbow, drinking Rob Roys in seedy bars, flirting with rough-looking men, hiding in closets at home, refusing to have sex with my husband. Also I mumbled my way through psychotherapy, having dreams, nightmares, I never reported to my therapist—knocking a Basilisk lizard off the rafters, presenting my dreams of houses to a Pharaoh, becoming divided into three persons, a murderer, a coward scrambling up the stairs, and finally I was a gallant figure galloping away on a large horse."

Paul chuckled, "I'm sure you were aware of how conflicted you were about your father's love for you and yours for him."

"No, no, I adored him!" she exclaimed chewing her sashimi fillet of salmon, savoring the fresh rawness with its taste of the seas, "He introduced me to the finer aspects of the world, ideas, imagination, aspiring towards the heavens, endeavoring to win the admiration of noble exalted beings."

Paul's small eyes narrowed into slits as he murmured, "But maybe this wasn't what you really wanted; maybe you wanted to find your own way, creating your very own agenda." He began to eat once again.

"Oh but I so wanted to become what he wanted, to be what he wished me to be!" Larana's face glowed, her wrinkles disappearing.

"Well, answer me this—did he ever appreciate anything about you that was not an extension of himself?"

"I can't think of any but why should I, it doesn't matter, I was content with his tutelage. Well, come to think of it I was shocked of how critical and disapproving he was of me, when, at twenty-four, I told him of my being diagnosed with rheumatoid arthritis."

"Aha!" Paul straightened up, sitting back in his chair with energy, "Maybe you were trying to separate from him by developing an imperfection!" After a pause, he continued, "It was your only way of tearing yourself away from his grasp—your battle against the disease became your very own quest."

"That's ridiculous! No on can bring on a disease at will!" Larana was impatient.

"Of course—we're only talking, conjecturing, using metaphors every which way, don't get upset!" Paul reached for her hand, holding it for a few seconds, but then withdrawing his hand as quickly as possible. They didn't speak for a long time.

"Still, there is something to what you're saying, well, at least about my father's personality—I'll never forget what he said at a celebration of my marriage to James. Embracing me, he whispered, his face close to mine, "We know what it is like to really love, don't we?" I remember not knowing why I felt so uncomfortable.

Paul's voice was soft, "In a way I feel for him; he wanted so badly not to be thrown to one side, maybe he was afraid he'd be forgotten. But you must see how possessive he was of you, how unheeding of your individuality."

Larana frowned, pressing some pieces of fresh ginger into her wasabi mustard, then eating it with fervor, relishing how it burned her mouth, throat and esophagus.

"Look, Paul began, "You mustn't mind me! But I've had years and years of psychoanalysis. I understand the plight of children having to be dependent on their parents for so many years!"

Larana coughed, then when she spoke her voice was deep, hoarse, "Yes, but you forget that this dependence can also provide a great opportunity for learning from experienced beings, from people who really care for you."

"Okay, okay, you're right—the teaching, the learning can sometimes be good," Paul said with reluctance.

"You're such a cynic. I don't dare ask what your growing up was like!"

"Please, don't ask!" Paul laughed loudly.

• • •

It was then that Larana had attempted to rise to her feet. It was time to leave the Japanese restaurant. It was three in the afternoon, its closing hour for lunch. It was then that something ruptured in one of her legs, making a popping sound, rendering her lame. Eventually Paul called 911 and while they waited she only laughed, finishing her sake, not realizing that in another realm of her being, she was slowly becoming transformed. She was changing into a kind of monster such as the one in Kafka's *Metamorphosis*, a monster perhaps conjured up as a giant 'sore thumb,' a beast 'thumbing its nose' at the world, a creature born violently as it tears itself free of a suffocating confinement.

The Mask of Thalassa

Thalassa had been around for a long time but he hadn't always been the man from the waterways, from the river near the hospital. However, in his many guises, he was never far from Larana. He wasn't stalking her; he never had to; she was always the one who called for him! In one instance, disguised as James, he stayed with her for almost thirty years. It's strange, but in a way, 'the other man' James always jealously feared, was right there within himself. Why did Larana need to call Thalassa forth in the first place, why did he heed her? Theirs was a dangerous necessary flirtation that was always balancing life and death, vibrancy and the loss of self, balancing love and solitude. She called Thalassa because she was in love with him. It had begun long before when she had stood on a cliff, aloof, remote, looking down at the sea pounding away at the rocks with such energy, such unceasing constancy. He was the perfect antidote for her aimlessness, her incertitude, especially from the age of seventeen to twenty-four—a young ever-scholarly husband and a few desultory affairs were far from satisfying.

Then one day when she was twenty-four, she went to

model for an artist. It turned out to be James.

"So, you've gone back to school to read writers like Albert Camus?" James asked during a rest period.

"Yes, his philosophy agrees with me, the idea that the end result of all efforts is of no importance, what matters is the beauty we can see while on our journey." Larana said this without knowing or feeling what she was saying—the words were merely comforting, seeming to come from nowhere, from a part of herself that was more mature than she actually was.

Larana loved watching James' face as he drew, using her face and body as inspiration—his high cheekbones becoming more prominent, his delicate nostrils flared, his smooth lips slightly parted. But above all, it was what happened to his eyes that fascinated her the most, the gray turning to violet, then a deep purple-brown, all the while looking pensive, far away, perhaps his being transported to a land of hills and tall trees. The drawings never looked like her. She thought she liked this; she thought she preferred to remain unattainable unpossessed. But then she also wasn't sure she liked being almost nonexistent, a nebular creature belonging nowhere, only a model being used by another.

James and Larana worked together for many months, meeting once a week for four hours. They continued to talk about novels, stories during the rest periods. The tale that moved them both the most was about the lioness and a soldier marooned in the desert. The lion took care of him and all that was expected of him was to trust that she would not hurt him. One day everything went terribly wrong—the man thought he saw her claws coming out, long, sharp; he thought she was beginning to bare her teeth, all her muscles tensing for a leap in his direction. He was petrified, he couldn't think. Instinctively, he drew his pistol and shot her dead. Larana thought she believed in trusting the goodness in the other, identifying with the innocent lioness, but, in reality, she felt more like the armed man.

That very day, as Larana was leaving James' studio, he reached for her, embracing her, kissing her fervently on the lips. As she was about to pull herself away despite liking the sweet silkiness of his lips, he himself drew away murmuring, "Don't tease me, please don't tease me!" His pained look made her turn her lips up to his saying, "I promise." But the quiver she felt passing through her whole being was that of fear, of an agonizing dread. Visualizing the image of the sea and its waves, she felt she'd known James and his embrace from way back in her life. She tightened her hold on him, wanting to crush him into her flesh, having his protective body infuse her with strength.

The next few sessions James behaved as if nothing had happened. She also was silent, even avoiding looking at him as he drew, even looking away when he attempted to show her his drawings of heroic-looking figures that were bigger than life.

Then, one day, he asked her to have lunch with him the following week, before the session, saying he would have the apartment all to himself. When the special day came as she prepared to leave her apartment she felt faint, throwing up her breakfast. Slowly she put on a red silk Russian tunic with a myriad of buttons. James met her at his door, his hair rumpled, his expression more tortured than ever, his hands trembling as he helped remove her coat, as he led her into the dining room. On the table were two crystal bowls and two crystal fluted goblets. Without a word he served a cold turtle soup and an even-colder champagne. Looking closely at him for the first time, beyond his face, she noticed he was wearing a Japanese kimono which fell open at the chest revealing a small patch of gray-brown fluff. She barely touched the soup but kept asking for more and more champagne, the bubbles stinging the inside of her mouth.

After the bottle was empty, James gently helped her to her feet and holding her by her arm he led her to the bedroom. Larana noticed the twin double beds. She had guessed he was married and during one of their sessions, heard the distant laughter of young children from the far end of the apartment. James sat her down on the edge of the nearest bed and embraced her lightly. Then drawing himself away, looking into her face he began to unbutton her tunic.

"Did you wear this on purpose?" he laughed.

"I'm not sure, perhaps," she smiled, feeling empowered by her alleged wickedness.

They spent many hours in bed sometimes not even lovemaking but just tumbling around, twisted around each other's sweaty flesh, breathing in the aroma of their diverse oils and milkiness. He confessed he was married, had two small children and that he'd never been unfaithful before. He added that he learned to love only after caring for his babies.

Larana asked, "Why should this be so?"

"I guess it's seeing how helpless, how vulnerable the little creatures are—seeing how innocently they depend on you," James whispered still clinging to her.

"Somehow there seems to be something wrong with loving only because someone is smaller, powerless, perhaps, one can say, inferior," Larana's voice was hesitant, as she too remained merged with him.

"I meant that the baby taught me *how* to love not *whom* to love!"

Once again the image of the sea returned fleetingly to her mind, the waves sweeping her off her feet, off the cliff top, encircling her, submerging her in its swirling mass. In all their subsequent time together, almost thirty years, she was never to reveal the imagery of the sea to James. Why? She didn't know.

In the end, many years later, James died of a congestive heart in their king-size bed, in their yellow bedroom, listening to Vivaldi's *Double Violin Concerto* while two tall candles burnt slowly all night long. Naked, she had crept up to his side, as close to his trembling flesh as she could get. By dawn his breathing was shallow, he seemed not to hear or sense the world. His last communication had been in the previous evening when he reached for her hand, caressing it with tepid fingers, murmuring "dear pussycat." Finally, that dawn, as the day's light greeted them, as it disrobed everything in the room, his chest rose upwards and never came down again. She waited—perhaps he was only holding his breath, but no, all movement had ceased. In time, as she remained up against him, all warmth disappeared, the still coldness pushing her away.

Thalassa had left long before the night of music and candles. Who knows where he went before he resurfaced in the river, near the hospital many years later. He no longer needed or wanted a disguise. Larana must come to know him for who he was. She must understand to whom she was calling.

Under the Knife

Finally awake, Larana opened her eyes. Looking around she saw an intravenous tube attached to one arm. Beyond the side rails of her bed, beyond her wide windows, the river no longer sent signals of light; it was as mute as an abyss. Raising her head a little, she saw that one of her legs was thickly swaddled in white, in sharp contrast to her memory of the surgeon who had been gowned in red. He had towered over her seeming to recede into a vast background, looking like a wound in the sky, his eyes burning into her like falling pieces of the sun. She winced, a deep pain coming from her leg. It was familiar. It was what she'd always felt after her previous surgeries. But now, ever since her recent rupture of a tendon, above one knee, leading to a long hospitalization in which infections ravaged her body, everything had been different; she'd lost both her old knee prosthetics, one leg had had to be fused, rendering it forever unbending and now a new prosthetic had been put in the other leg which may or may not remain without being infected. But the most unsettling difference was that these recent surgeries hadn't left her feeling fresh, renewed, cleansed. No, on the contrary, totally distraught, she'd sought to escape from the hospital, to plunge into the river, to drown herself; then she'd met the enigmatic Thalassa who turned out to have the same penetrating eyes as those of the red-garbed surgeon. Beginning to tremble from the effort of raising herself upwards, she let her head drop back onto her pillow. Her eyes had seen no one else in the room, her ears heard only distant noises in the hallway but she knew she was not alone.

Before long there he was, no longer masked, be-gloved, be-capped, still dressed in red but with a doctor's coat over it, a coat as black as his sweptback hair.

"I am not who you think I am!" he began in a deep rich voice," I am not Thalassa, I am not a creature of nature, fertility, life. I am myself, hating those who crumble at the thought of me, who cringe at my touch, who fall to the ground when I embrace and kiss them. You are different—you both want me and resist me."

Larana was barely audible, "You're wrong. I too, am scared to death."

Gripping the side rails he leaned forward, downwards, the bones of his gaunt face becoming more prominent. "Maybe, but you're excited by me. Throughout your life you've shown me how you yearn for the hide-and-seek game of seduction; you are enraptured by the lack of clarity, the incertitude, the agony of not knowing whether you're loved or not, even by me."

A voice hidden inside her shouted, "You're wrong; I'm different now." But she could only open her mouth, saying nothing.

The red and black image laughed so hard, the bed

shook, "Since you were a child you've needed to adore me in order to feel alive, flirting with me, flaunting your dangerous escapades in my face, always daring, taunting me."

Larana pushed her head hard into her pillow, nodding violently, as he continued, "You've always wanted me, not the sea but the sea demon from the caverns, the labyrinth, at the bottom of the ocean. Ask yourself, why don't aromatic flowers and soothing breezes seem inviting to you?"

Finally her voice returned but it was hoarse, croaky, "I do like them; it's just that they don't call out to me, they don't seek me out, encircling me."

"Of course, they're weak. You need to merge with power, with the powerful, no matter what it costs you."

Leaning down even further, his craggy face not far from hers, he continued, "Look how you have bloomed with every dramatic abandonment, every deadly intrusion into your being—you have gallantly leapt to one side, flown above it all, forever empathizing, forgiving, relishing the harm done unto you as long as you could exhibit your saintly heroism."

"But no more, no longer," her cheeks were aflame. After a few moments, she asked, "Who are you anyway?"

"Don't be coy; you know who I am; it is you who have called out to me; that is why I have come, this time to take you away at last."

"What could you possibly want with me? I'm just an old woman, a cripple."

"So much the better. I can finally carry you, take

care of you." He straightened up, smiling, his black eyes without any spots of light. Larana was reminded of what James had once said—that he had learned to love by taking care of his two infants. She remembered being dismayed by the idea that love could spring from the caring of the weak, the vulnerable, inferior beings, in a way, who could only wail, thrash about, soil themselves, demanding to be nourished. Now, as she faced the towering apparition, she remembered how her father had reacted to her announcement she'd been diagnosed with rheumatoid arthritis—his face had shown the pain of a deep disappointment, a humiliation, an insult as if she had been dethroned, as if he himself had been dethroned. Larana's swaddled leg began to hurt infinitely more sharply than before. She took many deep breaths—the pain would not subside. She shook her leg, commanding it to desist, but the pain was soon agonizing nonetheless, moans escaping from deep within her. Finally she yelled, "The hell with you, I hear you, I hear you!"

Avoiding looking at the apparition she looked at her swaddled leg with the new knee snuggled within. With her free arm and hand she stretched towards the white bundle, patting it, caressing it as it quivered a little, slightly rising up towards her warm fingers. With tears in her eyes, she turned to look at the spot where the costumed man had been. He was not there; it had faded away.

Spuyten Duyvil

Meeting Eyes Bindery

Triton

8th Avenue — Stefan Brecht
A Day and a Night at the Baths — Michael Rumaker
Acts of Levitation — Laynie Browne
Alien Matter — Regina Derieva
Anarchy — Mark Scroggins
Apo/Calypso — Gordon Osing
Apples of the Earth — Dina Elenbogen
Arc: Cleavage of Ghosts — Noam Mor
The Arsenic Lobster — Peter Grandbois
Auntie Varvara's Clients — Stelian Tanase
Balkan Roulette — Drazan Gunjaca
The Banks of Hunger and Hardship — J. Hunter Patterson
Black Lace — Barbara Henning
Bird on the Wing — Juana Culhane
Breathing Bolaño — Thilleman & Blevins
Breathing Free — (ed.) Vyt Bakaitis
Burial Ship — Nikki Stiller
Butterflies — Brane Mozetic
By The Time You Finish This Book You Might Be Dead — Aaron Zimmerman
Captivity Narratives — Richard Blevins
Celestial Monster — Juana Culhane
Cleopatra Haunts the Hudson — Sarah White
Columns: Track 2 — Norman Finkelstein
Consciousness Suite — David Landrey

The Conviction & Subsequent Life of Savior Neck — Christian TeBordo
Conviction's Net of Branches — Michael Heller
The Corybantes — Tod Thilleman
Crossing Borders — Kowit & Silverberg
Day Book of a Virtual Poet — Robert Creeley
The Desire Notebooks — John High
Detective Sentences — Barbara Henning
Diary of a Clone — Saviana Stanescu
Diffidence — Jean Harris
Donna Cameron — Donna Cameron
Don't Kill Anyone, I Love You — Gojmir Polajnar
Dray-Khmara as a Poet — Oxana Asher
Egghead to Underhoof — Tod Thilleman
The Evil Queen — Benjamin Perez
Extreme Positions — Stephen Bett
The Farce — Carmen Firan
Fission Among The Fanatics — Tom Bradley
The Flame Charts — Paul Oppenheimer
Flying in Water — Barbara Tomash
Form — Martin Nakell
Gesture Through Time — Elizabeth Block
Ghosts! — Martine Bellen
Giraffes in Hiding — Carol Novack
God's Whisper — Dennis Barone
Gowanus Canal, Hans Knudsen — Tod Thilleman
Half-Girl — Stephanie Dickinson
Hidden Death, Hidden Escape — Liviu Georgescu
Houndstooth — David Wirthlin
Identity — Basil King
In Times of Danger — Paul Oppenheimer

Incretion   Brian Strang

Inferno   Carmen Firan

Infinity Subsections   Mark DuCharme

Inverted Curvatures   Francis Raven

Jackpot   Tsipi Keller

The Jazzer & The Loitering Lady   Gordon Osing

Knowledge   Michael Heller

Lady V.   D.R. Popa

Last Supper of the Senses   Dean Kostos

A Lesser Day   Andrea Scrima

Let's Talk About Death   M. Maurice Abitbol

Light House   Brian Lucas

Light Years: Multimedia in the East Village, 1960-1966   (ed.) Carol Bergé

Little Book of Days   Nona Caspers

Little Tales of Family & War   Martha King

Long Fall: Essays and Texts   Andrey Gritsman

Lunacies   Ruxandra Cesereanu

Lust Series   Stephanie Dickinson

Lyrical Interference   Norman Finkelstein

Maine Book   Joe Cardarelli (ed.) Anselm Hollo

MANNHATTeN   Sarah Rosenthal

Meanwhile   Gordon Osing

Medieval Ohio   Richard Blevins

Memory's Wake   Derek Owens

Mermaid's Purse   Laynie Browne

Mobility Lounge   David Lincoln

The Moscoviad   Yuri Andrukhovych

Multifesto: A Henri d'Mescan Reader   Davis Schneiderman

No Perfect Words   Nava Renek

No Wrong Notes   Norman Weinstein

North & South Martha King
Notes of a Nude Model Harriet Sohmers Zwerling
Of All The Corners To Forget Gian Lombardo
Our Father M.G. Stephens
Over the Lifeline Adrian Sangeorzan
Part of The Design Laura E. Wright
Pieces for Small Orchestra & other fictions Norman Lock
A Place in the Sun Lewis Warsh
The Poet : Pencil Portraits Basil King
Political Ecosystems J.P. Harpignies
Powers: Track 3 Norman Finkelstein
Prurient Anarchic Omnibus j/j Hastain
Retelling Tsipi Keller
Rivering Dean Kostos
Root-Cellar to Riverine Tod Thilleman
The Roots of Human Sexuality M. Maurice Abitbol
Saigon and other poems Jack Walters
A Sardine on Vacation Robert Castle
Savoir Fear Charles Borkhuis
Secret of White Barbara Tomash
Seduction Lynda Schor
See What You Think David Rosenberg
Settlement Martin Nakell
Sex and the Senior City M. Maurice Abitbol
Slaughtering the Buddha Gordon Osing
The Snail's Song Alta Ifland
The Spark Singer Jade Sylvan
Spiritland Nava Renek
Strange Evolutionary Flowers Lizbeth Rymland
Suddenly Today We Can Dream Rutha Rosen

The Sudden Death of... Serge Gavronsky
The Takeaway Bin Toni Mirosevich
Talking God's Radio Show John High
Tautological Eye Martin Nakell
Ted's Favorite Skirt Lewis Warsh
Things That Never Happened Gordon Osing
This Guy James Lewelling
Thread Vasyl Makhno
Three Mouths Tod Thilleman
Three Sea Monsters Tod Thilleman
Track Norman Finkelstein
Transitory Jane Augustine
Transparencies Lifted From Noon Chris Glomski
Tsim-tsum Marc Estrin
Vienna ØØ Eugene K. Garber
Uncensored Songs for Sam Abrams (ed.) John Roche
Warp Spasm Basil King
Watchfulness Peter O'Leary
Walking After Midnight Bill Kushner
West of West End Peter Freund
When the Gods Come Home to Roost Marc Estrin
Whirligig Christopher Salerno
White, Christian Christopher Stoddard
Within the Space Between Stacy Cartledge
A World of Nothing But Self-Infliction Tod Thilleman
Wreckage of Reason (ed.) Nava Renek
the Yellow House Robin Behn
You, Me, and the Insects Barbara Henning

Made in the USA
Middletown, DE
15 November 2020